Zombie Diaries
Winter Formal Junior Year
The Mavis Saga

By
R.W.K. Clark

This is a work of fiction. All names, characters, locales, and incidents are
the product of the author's imagination and any resemblance to actual
people, places or events is coincidental or fictionalized.
Published in the United States by Clarkltd.
Po Box 45313 Rio Rancho, NM 87174
info@clarkltd.com

Edition 1

United States Copyright Office
#TX 8-425-978 April 2017
Library of Congress Control Number: 2017907165
International Standard Book Numbers
ISBN-10: 0997876786
ISBN-13: 978-0997876789
ASIN: B072XV89T7

/200801

ZOMBIE DIARIES SERIES

Zombie Diaries - Homecoming Junior Year - ZD1
ISBN-10: 0997876778 ISBN-13: 978-0997876772

Zombie Diaries - Winter Formal Junior Year - ZD2
ISBN-10: 0997876786 ISBN-13: 978-0997876789

Zombie Diaries - Prom Junior Year - ZD3
ISBN-10: 0997876794 ISBN-13: 978-0997876796

Zombie Diaries - Summer Break Junior Year - ZD4
ISBN-10: 1948312034 ISBN-13: 978-1948312035

Zombie Diaries - Fall Semester Senior Year - ZD5
ISBN-10: 1948312042 ISBN-13: 978-1948312042

Zombie Diaries - Senior Graduation - ZD6
ISBN-10: 1948312050 ISBN-13: 978-1948312059

CONTENTS

ACKNOWLEDGMENTS

I dedicate this novel to my wonderful readers and for all the amazing people I've met and those I haven't. To my family and loved ones, all your support will not be forgotten.

This book was made possible by reviews from readers like you.

Thank you

R.W.K. Clark

CHAPTER 1

Mavis Harvey sat beneath the stars in her mother's favorite patio chair. It was a chilly October night, and Mavis could just barely see her breath each time she exhaled. The evening was clear and crisp, almost invigorating, and Mavis loved to just sit and enjoy the peace and quiet.

Her parents, Jane and Todd, were out with friends, which they frequently did at least once a week. Sometimes they played cards: other times they went dancing. They always enjoyed the company of other couples, and they would top off whatever weekend activity they participated in with a nice dinner. They wouldn't be home until late, Mavis knew.

Just a couple of months ago, Mavis had dreaded the setting-in of the cold. She had never been one to enjoy winter, or building snowmen, or even indulging in the traditional sledding or snowball fights like other teens her age. But now things were different. She actually enjoyed the cold and felt that it was something of a refuge. She could handle the low temperatures without even thinking about it. She was sure that, as the season progressed, this would change and she would bundle up a bit more, but for now, the forty degrees she was sitting in was almost akin to being in her mother's womb, at least to Mavis.

So, it was strange, but many things were odd when it came to Mavis. She hadn't been the same girl she used to be for a couple of months, but especially since Jeff Deason, her first boyfriend ever had been killed. She missed him and wondered what could have been if she hadn't changed so drastically. Well, more appropriately, if she hadn't eaten him.

But, she had. The act, no matter how 'accidental,' wore on her mind and heart like a massive boulder. The emotions she carried with her on a daily basis had changed Mavis' entire disposition and attitude toward life, but she didn't really see it the way those around her did. But that didn't matter to her; they were just concerned that she might be taking Jeff's death too hard, and they were right. But, unbeknownst to anyone else, she had her own reasons; eating your boyfriend is enough to make any human being feel a bit weighed down.

A chilly wind hit her, and Mavis closed her eyes and lifted her face to it so she could feel it fully. It was cleansing, both physically and emotionally. She was so thankful that her parents were gone so she could be herself. Since she had first gotten 'sick,' everyone doted on her; from her parents and friends all the way to Dr. Meadows. He had even gone so far as to suggest sending her to the Mayo Clinic at their last visit. Her pale skin was what pushed him over the edge, but Mavis had refused. She insisted to her parents that she felt physically fine: she was energetic, mentally sharp, and even stronger than ever. Because of those obvious things, they had let go of the nagging, at least for the time being, and the Mayo Clinic was put on the back burner.

Her next obstacle consisted of her mother wanting her to go tanning three times a week to bring her skin tone back to normal. Mavis wanted no part of it for a couple of reasons: first, it wasn't good for you to make a habit out of lying in a sunbed; science proved it every day. Second, she had come to like the way she looked, all ghostly and stuff. It had grown on her like a fungus. It didn't bother her a bit.

Here was the best news of all, at least to Mavis, as no one else was aware: she had been controlling her urges to eat others like a pro, ever since the incident with her accidentally eating Jeff Deason. Mavis now pretty much lived on raw liver, morning, noon, and night, and it helped take the edge off when she was overcome with temptation. She'd had to learn that she couldn't limit herself to snacking on the bloody meat only two or three times a day; she had to do it whenever the urge came. This involved taking her little cooler with her pretty much wherever she went, and it also involved excusing herself to go to the bathroom at least once during every class. The funny thing was, because of her appearance and the concern of doctors, her teachers had no problem allowing it. Her parents had even sat through a meeting with the principal and extended their daughter permission to be able to leave classes frequently due to her 'ailment.' Mavis maintained top-notch grades, so the school cooperated in full, all for her 'well-being.' She laughed when she thought about it.

Another breeze swept through, this one stronger and more insistent. For the first time, Mavis got a slight chill, and it felt good. She knew that she wouldn't be outside much longer. A quick glance at her cell phone screen told her it was just after nine, and she wanted to call her best friend, Kim Coleman before it got too late. Kim was on a date with her boyfriend of more than two months, Shawn Maher. Shawn had been Jeff's good friend, and he had been instrumental in hooking the pair up. Mavis found it ironic, and it made her sad to think about it.

But with all that put aside, she was still Kim's best friend, and after every date, the two girls would chatter about all the details. It might have made Mavis sad to go through it each and every time, but she loved her friend like a sister, and Kim needed her to do those things, just like she had needed Kim like that when she and Jeff first started dating. She refused to let her lifelong sidekick down.

Mavis stood and let herself in through the sliding glass door off the dining room. She was followed by a gust of cold air, and she even hesitated so she could let a little bit more of it in. After a moment, she slid the door slowly closed, a sad smile on her face. Oh, well; she would crack her bedroom window while she slept, and that would make up for it.

She made her way back to her room. Mavis sat down at her vanity and placed her cell down beside her, so she would be sure not to miss Kim's call. Next, she flipped on the small lamp which sat on the vanity, and she began to gaze intently at her reflection.

Her long, brown hair seemed to be getting much darker she had noticed. Even her mother, Jane, had made several comments about it. It was still shiny and held the large curls that hung down her back very well, but for some reason, it seemed to be bordering on black. Mavis thought about the box of dye she had picked up at Carl's Thrifty Nickel last week, and as she looked at herself, her decision became firm: she would use that dye tonight. She was actually beginning to like the way the darkness of her hair made her pasty skin look: more like porcelain than paste. Yes, the dye was the solution.

Mavis sat back and continued to study herself. The red which rimmed her eyes didn't bother her in the slightest, but it made others constantly comment that she looked feverish. She had taken to using much eyeliner and mascara to cover up the redness, and Mavis also thought that the choice complemented her hue. As a matter of fact, for all the things that had been going on in her life, and all the painful changes that had been taking place, she thought she looked like a million bucks… almost hot, as the boys liked to say.

Not that it mattered. Mavis steered clear of the opposite sex, and she had been doing so ever since Jeff Deason's unfortunate murder. No, Mavis would not be dating any time soon, and that bummed her out immensely. She liked boys very much, but she couldn't risk eating each and every guy who asked her out. If she did that, the suburb where she lived would be at a very real risk of running out of the boy population. Besides, she didn't want to wind up in some insane asylum, or worse yet, prison.

Tired of looking at herself, Mavis rose and went to her bed and flopped down. She laid her cell next to her and then grabbed the remote from her nightstand. Nothing better to do than watch some television. It was only nine forty, and Kim wouldn't be calling until eleven or so. After all, it was Saturday night, and no teenager on a date, who was in her right mind, went home any earlier than she could get away with. So, Mavis began to channel surf as she gave a big, lonely sigh.

CHAPTER 2

"Hey, I'm glad you called." Mavis glanced at the clock on her nightstand: eleven thirty. "I was nearly asleep; you almost missed me."

Kim gave a chuckle. "You better have answered, or you'd have had me to answer to, and you don't want that!"

The girls both laughed, then Mavis gave a huge yawn, which she tried to stifle. "How are you feeling, Mav?" Kim asked.

"Like usual," she replied. "Tired, but that's mostly boredom. So, fill me in: how was the date, girl?"

"Like usual," Kim mimicked playfully. "Ah, you know, pretty typical. I have quickly learned that Shawn is a creature of habit, just like you and me. Our date was pretty much identical to last week, with miniature golf instead of a cheesy movie, and Sports Burger. I loved it. I'm crazy about him!"

Mavis smiled at her friend's contentment and joy. "I know you are, and I'm glad. Next date?"

"Next Friday night," Kim stated. "He has to put in extra practice time on Saturday because the coach says he needs to focus more since he was promoted to the quarterback. You know, to take… Jeff's place." Her voice drifted off.

Mavis closed her eyes and ignored the pain in her heart. "It's okay, Kim. I'm working on getting over it. You don't have to walk on eggshells for me; you're my sister, you know."

"That's why I do." Mavis could hear the girl taking a deep breath. "Anyway, on a more cheerful note, we made out in my driveway for so long that my dad came out in his pajamas with a baseball bat. Wish you could have seen it! Shawn nearly jumped out of his own car and ran up the block!"

Mavis began to laugh hysterically, and Kim right along with her. The thought of Richard Coleman in Buckeye pajamas, swinging a ball bat while the moon shone off his bald head, was more than she could bear. Mr. Coleman was an anxious man, and he was prone to making mountains out of molehills, especially when it came to his only daughter.

When she gained control of herself, Mavis asked. "Was your mom there? Did she do anything?"

"Yeah," Kim said. "She stood in the doorway in her robe yelling, 'Dick, if you don't get back in bed and leave those kids alone I'm going to use that bat on you!' It was crazy. I nearly peed my pants. That was the first time Shawn got to see my dad in overdrive, so I'm pretty sure he did pee his pants! Aw, it was too much!"

"I wish I could have been a squirrel under a bush; what a riot, Kim." Mavis had to wipe tears of laughter from her eyes.

Kim gave another sigh, this one filled with sleepiness. "Well, Mav. I'm gonna go; I'm wiped out. Have you done your calculus yet?"

"Yep; Friday night, slowpoke."

Kim groaned. "And you're going to Grandma Cabot's tomorrow?"

"Mm-hmm," Mavis replied.

"So, I'll be over in the morning after breakfast so you can help me," she said quickly. "Love ya. See you then!"

She hung up before Mavis could argue, but she didn't mind. Kim struggled with math. Mavis always wound up bailing her out.

She hooked up her phone to the charger and rose to open the window. Mavis then crawled in bed and turned off the TV and lamp. She was afraid she wouldn't sleep; sometimes memories of Jeff would keep her up for a while.

But, fortunately for Mavis, she was out nearly as soon as she closed her eyes.

∞

"Mavis, breakfast is ready!"

The sudden interruptive sound of Jane Harvey screaming down the hallway at her daughter caused Mavis to nearly jump out of her pale skin. Having risen extra-early, she had just finished blow-drying and styling her freshly-dyed black hair, and it looked amazing. Sure, she'd had to get up at five-thirty on a Sunday to get it done, but she had managed to do it without rousing her sleeping parents.

Mavis stood and gave herself one last look: she wore black skinny jeans tucked into boots and a black sweater. The addition of silver earrings, bangle bracelets, and a necklace set the outfit off perfectly. As for her makeup, she wore no foundation, blush, or powder; her skin was porcelain-white and sparkling-clear. All she did was add black eyeliner and mascara. With her new hair color, Mavis thought she looked beautiful.

Now, to find out what her mother would say about her new look.

She grabbed her cell phone and made her way to the kitchen. Breakfast smelled great, even though she had already eaten two pieces of raw liver. Mavis was getting used to being hungry all the time, and she had adapted well. The meat was a necessity; her mother's meals were icing on the cake, much like fine desserts.

Turning the corner, she walked into the kitchen and exclaimed, "Voilà!"

Jane was standing at the stove putting bacon on a paper-towel-lined plate. She had a smile on her face, but only until she turned to look at her daughter. Then it quickly faded. Her eyes grew a bit wider, and she froze with her fork in the air.

"D-D-Did you... dye it, Mavis?" Jane put the plate and fork on the counter absentmindedly, then turned and started toward her. She reached out and took hold of one of the long, curly locks gently. "But it makes you look so... so... so white! I thought we were going to wait on this."

Mavis shrugged and turned away, making her way to

her place setting and the food and milk waiting there for her. "I changed my mind," she said simply as she sat down. "I love it, Mom. It will grow on you; I promise."

Jane just stood there and stared for a moment as Mavis dug into her breakfast. She ignored her mother's eyes for several minutes, but when she could take it no more, she swallowed a bite and looked up. "Yes? Mother?"

The woman shook her head quickly as if trying to clear it. "Sorry." Jane went back to the bacon plate. "I guess I just... I loved your natural color so much."

"It was getting darker fast, and it looked crappy like my roots were showing or something." Mavis scooped up another bite. "Besides, it makes me feel good."

Jane finished up at the stove and sat at the table across from Mavis. "It doesn't look bad; don't get me wrong. You're a beautiful girl. But you kind of look like one of those... heavy metal, or punk, rockers."

Mavis made a face. "Get real. It's me, Mom."

Jane took a sip of her coffee, then made her own face and stood to warm it up. "What are your plans today?"

Mavis spoke around a mouthful of food. "Kim's coming; calculus." It sounded like 'Kins cornin callous.' Jane gave her a confused look, so she swallowed and repeated the phrase.

"Well, don't forget Grandma's today," Jane said. "She's going to die when she sees you." The woman took her coffee cup and left the kitchen.

Mavis was relieved to finish her food in peace. For a

parent who always pushed for her to eat with her mouth closed, she sure asked a lot of questions. Now she could finish without the third degree or anymore scrutinizing looks.

As soon as she had cleaned her second plate, Mavis focused on loading the dishwasher and straightening things up in the kitchen. She hoped that her assistance would motivate her mom to get off the hair kick. She managed to get the task done in no time, and just as she was starting the washer, she heard the doorbell: Kim.

Mavis went to greet her friend. As soon as Kim saw her, she gave Mavis the same reaction Jane had: open mouth and eyes, and stunned silence.

"It was getting darker anyway!" Mavis said with exasperation. "Jeesh!"

Kim pulled herself together. "Darker, yes. But you look like some kind of vampire or something."

Mavis stuck her tongue out. "I like it, so shut up. Do you need help with homework, or did you come here to interview me for a magazine's beauty editorial?"

"Sorry." Kim turned to Jane. "I won't take up much of her time."

The girls went to Mavis' room, where they always studied. Once inside and settled, Kim started to open her mouth, but Mavis stopped her. She knew it was going to be about the hair again.

"Don't," she said simply and firmly, holding up her hand.

Kim shrugged. "I guess it will just take some getting used to."

"Exactly."

Mavis spent the next hour tutoring her pal and helping her struggle through her homework. When they were finished, she ran out and grabbed a couple of sodas and some cookies from the jar. She then returned to her room to chat with Kim.

"So," the girl began as soon as Mavis closed the bedroom door. "Shawn and I are already planning for the Winter Formal."

Mavis didn't answer; she just shoved a cookie into her mouth, so Kim continued.

"Um… are you going?"

Mavis chewed her cookie and swallowed, then shook her head. "I doubt it. I mean, this is your time, you know?"

"Shawn says a number of the guys want to ask you, but they're nervous." She was playing with a cookie. "You know, because of Jeff."

Mavis peered at her. "What do you mean, 'because of Jeff'?"

"They're just afraid you're still kind of… you know, mourning or something."

She took a long drink of soda. "I am. So?"

"Well," Kim continued. "Wouldn't you want to go if you had a date? I mean, we could shop for dresses together and stuff, just like always."

Mavis leaned back against her vanity. "Look, Kim. A lot has happened. Don't get me wrong; I'm not done with boys. I just need more time."

Kim nodded and stood up, handing her cookie to

Mavis. "I'd better get going. Mom wants me to help her change the living room around." She gathered her books up, then turned to Mavis, who was still sitting on the floor. "Just think about it. Not just for me, but for you."

"I will. See you later."

"Later," Kim replied, and she left the room.

Mavis looked at the cookie in her hand and noticed that her appetite was gone. Why did Kim have to go and bring up the dance? Just the thought of dating made her sick, especially when she wanted to eat people and had to fight the urge constantly.

Besides, who really wanted to date her? No one had, until Jeff, so why would they now? No, she would bide her time. When she was ready, she would know. All she knew right now was that, as long as they all smelled like fresh prime rib, she was going to keep her distance.

She got up and lay down on her bed, flipping the TV on as she did. One thing Mavis had discovered: there was no better way to forget your problems than to turn on the boob tube. It would drown out the worst, most torturous of thoughts.

So, Mavis let herself escape for a little while.

CHAPTER 3

With the dawning of the sun, Mavis was wide awake and, after some liver with lemon juice (a new idea), she was going through her closet to choose what she would wear that day. She felt excited about getting ready, for the first time in a while. Mavis didn't care what Kim, her parents, or even her grandmother, for that matter, thought about it; she felt attractive, and it was good.

She chose a black, form-fitting skirt that fell about two inches above her knee, a black poet's shirt with over-long bell sleeves, and her long-time favorite: freshly-polished black combat boots. She topped it off with a dressy trench coat and lots of jewelry. Eye makeup on and a hair-brush later, and Mavis stood before the mirror smiling.

She loved it. It was her, through and through. In her mind, Mavis knew she had slowly but surely been coming to this, and her mother was going to blow a fuse. The hair dyeing was what pushed her over the edge, and she was glad. Her mother was going to have to cope because she looked great.

A little… off, but great.

With laptop and book bags on her shoulder and the

little cooler full of the liver in hand, Mavis took a deep breath, opened the door with determination, and walked to the kitchen to have her breakfast.

Mavis turned into the kitchen, smiling big, and said, "Good mo…"

That was all she got out of her mouth. Her mother took one look at her, screamed at the top of her lungs, and tossed two plates of food directly into the air. Jane's scream was one of the longest on record, certainly; it flowed from her throat like a raging river filled with fury and disbelief. There was no fear in the piercing shriek, only the clearness of the woman's murderous anger. Mavis' smile disappeared in an instant.

A fraction of a second later, Jane's scream cut off all at once. Shards of broken plates were scattered all over the floor, among what appeared to be random piles of chunky yellow mush that looked like it might have been potatoes, eggs, and cheese at one time. Mavis thought maybe with bacon or sausage too, from the looks of it. She was distracted by the food and didn't even notice her mother had gone silent.

When Jane spoke, her voice was low, still, and threateningly serious.

"Are you auditioning for something today, Mavis?"

Mavis immediately tore her eyes from the floor and looked at her mom. "What?" she asked.

Jane took a deep breath, her steely gaze never shifting from Mavis; she scanned her daughter up and down, again and again, pausing only on her face. "Well, now, when you walked out here I saw you and thought to myself, 'Mavis must be trying out for drama, or maybe her class is having a Halloween party.' That's why you're all crazy-looking, right?"

Mavis had to control herself so she wouldn't panic. Nope, Mom wasn't taking it well at all. She was tempted to lie, but then she'd be sneaking to dress the way she wanted, and fighting, too. No, this had to be dealt with now.

"No, Mom," she said slowly. Mavis put her cooler against the wall and placed her bag on top. "I'll help you clean up." Mavis began to pick up the broken shards from the floor.

Jane stood, frozen. "What do you mean, no? No party, or no audition?"

Mavis tossed a handful of pieces into the garbage. "No nothing." She looked up to meet her mother's eyes. "This is what I'm wearing to school."

"Get up," Jane said abruptly. "Put that... mess... down, and get up!"

Without a second thought, Mavis dropped what she had in her hands and stood to her feet. Her mother was pissed, there was no doubt about it, and Mavis understood why. She had never dressed this way; Mavis had always been an average girl. Down-to-Earth, but a bright, chipper girl at heart. Her wardrobe had always reflected it.

But in the last couple of months, her taste had simply been... shifting. She didn't consider it a negative thing. Sure, the style didn't immediately convey the wholesome 'girl-next-door' image right away, but she carried herself with confidence, and she didn't walk around talking about suicide or how life is a drag.

The new style choice simply felt more like… her, the way she was at that moment.

"Sit at the table… no! Stand. I want to be face to face, and I can't sit right now." Jane shifted her weight from one foot to the other and crossed her arms over her chest. "Now, what is this about?"

Mavis shrugged; be honest, be honest. "Well, I guess this appeals to me. I think I look awesome."

She went through multiple eye scans once again. "I'm not saying you're not attractive, but it's a bit morbid, and not you at all. Are you depressed, Mavis? Are you on drugs? No, wait, please don't tell me you are thinking about suicide!"

Jane grabbed her by the shoulders and put her face an inch in front of her daughter's. Mavis couldn't help it; she broke out laughing, which really set Jane off. She gave her daughter a slug in the arm… a hard one.

"You're not funny! This is scary! This kind of change is scary to a parent, to a mother or father, Mavis!" Suddenly, Jane sat down at the table, as if all of her energy left her at once. Her face, for a split second, looked exhausted, and she shook her head. "Mavis, you may not be aware, but when this anemia thing set in, I had worries. Your physical appearance changed so quickly it petrified me. Now, for the last two months we have visited Dr. Meadows over and over, then the dermatologist. Oh, it's a pigment problem. You won't go to another doctor and insist you are fine. You act like you feel good. But you look like death; and, you dress like a corpse at a funeral." Jane was getting ready to cry.

"What's the matter with you? You think the last two months haven't affected me? I hardly sleep at night, Mavis."

The doorbell rang, and Mavis gave her mother a glance. "That will be Kim," she said without moving.

"Well, answer it, but tell her to go on without you." Jane shot her a look. "We aren't finished here yet."

So, Mavis went to the door and explained to her friend, who seemed shocked at her appearance but said nothing. Mavis told Kim that she and her mother were running late. Mavis told her she would see her in second period Science, then closed the door and returned to her lecture.

Jane ran her hand through her hair when she came back, and Mavis sat down. "Mom, my grades are some of the best in school. I eat like a horse. Sure, I may be grieving over Jeff, but you have to let me. I'm not suicidal; as a matter of fact, far from it. I just feel good the way I'm dressed. I'm not going to likely ease up. I promise, I'm not on drugs, and I'm in no way depressed. I love you." Mavis paused and stood up and struck a pose. "Besides… I look good."

Jane gave her a sideways glance, catching a dazzling smile; she began to grin herself. 'Yeah, you do. You jerk. What I'd give to be your age again."

Mavis pulled her mother to her feet, and they embraced. "Work on Grandma, will you? She handled my hair okay, I guess, after the lecture, anyway. But this might… you know."

Jane growled.

"Trust me, Mom?"

She looked her in the eyes. "Yes, I do."

They cleaned up the kitchen and settled on cold cereal. Mavis ate two bowls before she realized she was already late for school by fifteen minutes. Her mother called her in late, and after she ate, she hit the road.

She took her time walking. The streets were cleared of people, and leaves were falling all around, causing her to want to take her time; besides, she was late already. Mavis inhaled the brisk air and soaked up the serenity. Once she got to school, she would have to break in her peers to her new appearance, and Mavis was well aware of what a task that would be.

But hopefully, her new look would scare off some of the guys that had tried, so tirelessly, to ask her out since Jeff… went away.

CHAPTER 4

Mavis was right: her first day to school as her brand-new, comfortable self, proved to be just as interesting as she had expected it to be.

When she got to school, the first thing she had to do was go directly into the office. Even though her mother had called her in, she wouldn't be able to attend class without a pass from the secretary. This would be the perfect opportunity to see how the adults in her life, other than her mother, would react. She had forgotten about facing her father, but pushed that out of her mind quickly; this was enough for now.

Mavis approached the door with apprehension but took every step. In slow motion, her hand reached out and took hold of the door handle, then let herself into the office. Everything remained in slow motion after that.

The secretary looked up, followed by three other office women behind her. The room, which had been full of computer clicking and chatter when she opened the door, went dead silent. The door slammed closed loudly behind her.

"Mavis, is that you? What in the world…" Mrs.

Benson, the secretary, was staring at her in wonder.

"Um… well, it's like this. My skin has gotten all pale, as you all know, and all the makeup I was putting on was bad for my skin." She looked at each of the women one at a time, a pleasant smile on her face to cover the frustration she felt at their rudeness. "Anyway, this is my solution. I feel good." Mavis paused for effect. "And I look good too. No, I'm not depressed or on drugs. Can we just keep all this between us, for crying out loud?"

All the women broke into nervous laughter. Mrs. Benson was the first to apologize. "It was such a shock, the complete opposite of how we have always seen you. I'm sorry we froze. And… yes, it suits you."

The women in the rear all exchanged glances, and Mavis shot them a sarcastic smirk. "I just need a pass, Mrs. Benson. My mother called me in late."

The secretary set about filling out the pass while the other workers began tapping furiously on their keyboards. Mavis thought about their reactions and rolled her eyes. Man, she wasn't trying to shock everybody, or get attention. She just wanted to be herself, no matter what.

She knew she had a very interesting day ahead.

∞

Miss Hawkins, Mavis' Literature teacher, would be the next adult in her life to see her new look. This particular educator was the one Mavis had the most concern about. For one thing, she happened to be one of Miss Hawkins' favorite pupils; for another, she had a little incident a couple of months back when she had first gotten 'sick' while in Lit class that had caused a bit of a rift between them for a short time.

She made her way to her locker to put away her cooler and remembered. Mavis had gone to class one day right around the time Dr. Meadows told her she had low iron or 'anemia.' One of the symptoms she was suffering from, besides the pale skin, was the intense and constant starvation that she was still dealing with now. But then, however, she had not really gotten a handle on it.

As she walked to class, she recalled the situation in full. She had been sitting in class, and the hunger had begun. As a matter of fact, it had been torturing her somewhat. It had seemed that she could smell food all around her. Now, at that point, she had been dealing with it long enough to realize that she was smelling the flesh of her peers, and it was driving her mad. It had been the first period of the day, and Mavis had known, even then, that she wasn't going to make it until lunchtime.

That was when she noticed that the boy sitting next to her, Tommy Johnson, had a sack lunch in the book rack beneath his seat. Mavis tried to talk him into selling it to her by whispering and wheeling and dealing; she even offered him ten bucks! Miss Hawkins scolded them at one point for talking, but that didn't stop Mavis and her uncontrollable appetite. She tried again to convince the boy, and when he wouldn't submit, she grabbed the paper bag of food and ran from the room.

She bolted to the girls' room, where she locked herself in a stall and began to tear like a savage at the peanut butter and jelly sandwich the boy had brought. It was right there, with food on her face, that Mavis was discovered by a furious Miss Hawkins, accompanied by a confused and frustrated Principal Pearson. She was given an extra assignment (and a severe scolding, along with the need to rebuild trust) by Miss Hawkins, and two-day suspension from Mr. Pearson. Thinking back on it, Mavis couldn't help but smile. What the heck had she been thinking?

Now she stood in front of Miss Hawkins' classroom door. It wouldn't be only Miss Hawkins who would be surprised at her appearance, but her first-period class would be the first of her fellow students to get a load of the new Mavis. She couldn't care less what they thought, but she hoped that Miss Hawkins didn't look at her in too negative a light. She did like and respect the young woman.

Mavis turned the knob and walked in; everyone turned to look at her, including Miss Hawkins at the dry erase board. Mavis smiled at everyone and started for her teacher, whose mouth was slightly open. If a pin had hit the floor right then it would have sounded like a bomb going off, it was so quiet.

But she didn't say a word. Instead, she approached Miss Hawkins and handed her the pass. "Sorry I'm late; I had some personal family business to deal with at home."

She turned and walked directly to her desk, smiling

at every eye she met. She sat down and got situated, knowing that Miss Hawkins' eyes were still on her. Mavis didn't want to look up yet, so she fiddled with her pencil and concentrated on her fingernails, thinking maybe they would look good painted black with white tips.

Finally, Miss Hawkins snapped out of it. "As you all know, our focus of study this semester is the plot. So far, you have read a few books, and you have written detailed reports on each. Now, your final reading assignment concerning plot will be *Brother's Keeper*. If I read the reports you turn in on this book, and find myself suspicious that you watched the movie, you will be failed." She paused and looked slowly at her students. "I know that several of you did this with *Passage of Time*, and your report grade reflected my suspicions. Please, keep in mind that every book I assign, I have read, and I have also watched the films. The movies are always different in ways; you will be caught."

Miss Hawkins pointed to a couple of piles of books sitting on the small table next to her desk. "Rosa, would you do the honors?"

Rosa Hernandez stood and began to pass out the books. "Start reading today, in class. Reports will be due on December 2nd, and midterm testing will focus wholly on this author and the works by him which I have assigned. It will not be easy!"

Rosa dropped a book on Mavis' desk, and Mavis smiled pleasantly. She saw a small smile tugging at the corners of the girl's lips. She mouthed, "I like your hair!" Then tugged at a strand of her own to clarify. Mavis mouthed back, 'Thank you!'

The class began to settle in, and Mavis was already relaxed and reading. She had glanced around once to see a couple of smiles from other kids, and she reciprocated. It made her feel better, and she was able to focus.

"Mavis, could I have a word with you please? In the hall?"

It was Miss Hawkins.

Mavis didn't hesitate. She stood immediately, letting Miss Hawkins pass her desk, then followed the woman out the door. Once it was closed behind them, she turned to the teacher and waited patiently.

It took the woman a moment to speak as if she were weighing her words. "Mavis, are you okay?"

She just smiled and nodded. "I'm great! I feel better than I have since… you know."

Miss Hawkins smiled sympathetically. "Good. You're beginning to get over Jeff's passing. But… are the clothes—are you…?"

"I'm not depressed or on drugs, if that's what you mean," Mavis interrupted. "I guess I have always liked this style, and it helps with my paleness… you know. More… complimentary, I guess, that's all."

Miss Hawkins breathed a sigh of relief. "Well, it's different; a drastic change. But I have to admit, you look good. Striking, almost."

"Thank you."

With her teacher appeased, the two went back into the classroom, staring eyes all around. Mavis simply smiled and went back to the book. She was relieved that Miss Hawkins had been so understanding.

Finally, she could begin to be herself.

R.W.K. Clark

CHAPTER 5

"I mean, yeah, it's different, but you actually look pretty amazing."

Kim and Mavis walked home from school, discussing the new look that had managed to turn heads and steal everyone's attention all day. They had time to talk earlier between classes and at lunch, but nothing intense. Now, they were busy discussing the reactions of their peers.

Mavis had been more than surprised. Everyone had something to say, and none of it was bad. Kids she had never met had paid her compliments, and more than once she had to dodge looks from various boys. If she thought her look would put them off, she soon knew she was wrong.

"I like it! My mother came apart at the seams." Mavis smiled at the recollection.

Kim snorted. "I can imagine. So, is this just for today, or what?"

"Actually, I made myself over. This is the new me." Mavis stopped and spun around. "It fits me. It fits how I feel, and it fits my skin tone. To be honest, I think I'm beautiful for the first time in my life."

"You do look good," Kim replied in a jealous tone. "And did you see the way the guys were gawking?"

Mavis' smile faded, and she started walking again. "I don't care about them. Not right now, anyway."

Kim growled. 'What are you going to do? Never date? Grow up and be an old spinster?"

"Maybe." She picked up her pace. "It just doesn't matter right now. Just drop it, Kim. It'll pass."

When they got to Mavis' door, Kim said, "Well, at least you don't have to deal with your mom again."

"Ha! No, just my dad when he gets home."

Both girls groaned.

"So, do you wanna come in?" Mavis asked.

Kim shook her head. "Nah. I'm going with my mom to my brother's wrestling meet. We're leaving at five, and we won't be home until super-late. See you tomorrow?"

The girls parted ways, and Mavis went inside. Her mind was on getting a moment alone; she was feeling drained and really needed some liver. Kim had started to smell a bit like a cheeseburger, and Mavis was glad that she hadn't accepted the invitation to come inside.

"Mom, I'm home!"

There was a pause, then, "In the dining room, Mav!"

The dining room? Her mother never hung out in the dining room; heck, they didn't even eat in there unless they had company. Mavis shrugged, took her cooler and bag to her room, then went to join her mother.

Before she even got to the kitchen, she heard the voice of Grandma Cabot, and she winced. That's why her mother was in the dining room. Grandma Cabot didn't come over often, but when she did, she insisted on having coffee in the dining room. Bracing herself, Mavis crossed through the kitchen, her shoulders back and chin up.

"Hi, Mom. Hi, Grandma." She plopped down in an empty chair and waited expectantly.

Grandma Cabot looked her up and down. "Well, aren't we a brave, daring soul today."

Mavis gave her mother a glance, but Jane simply pretended to be folding cloth napkins. Mavis knew she was faking it because there was only one left to fold, and Jane had already folded and unfolded it once, then began again. Well, here goes, she thought.

"No, not daring," she said hesitantly. "Just… needed a change, Grandma."

"Hmmpf." Grandma Cabot adjusted herself in her chair and crossed her arms. "How do you think you look?"

Mavis shrugged. "I like it. Kim likes it too, and considering the fact that if I lay down in a snow drift, you would lose me, this is the right style for me."

"You look like Wednesday Addams," Marguerite Cabot said flatly. "But whatever. Don't you want to look like a nice, respectable girl?"

Mavis curled her lip. "I am a nice respectable girl."

"But don't you want to look like one?"

Now she was getting frustrated, and she was afraid she would say something stupid or disrespectful. She continued to make eye contact with her grandmother,

her mind racing to find the right words. After a moment, she got it.

"You know, I know girls in school who dress like nice, respectable girls." She made little quote signs with her fingers. "Some of them are failing classes, others do drugs, and Maryann Foster is pregnant!" She gave her mother a glance, then continued. "It seems to me that dressing like a 'nice, respectable girl' has become nothing more than a cover-up for being the exact opposite. At least with me, you get the opposite. I look good, Grandma; I don't care what anyone says. Are we done?"

Jane interrupted. "Maryann Foster is pregnant?"

Mavis groaned. "Yes. Her parents even took her out of school, and they don't even know who the father is."

The two older women gave each other shocked looks, but they didn't continue the grilling. Mavis stood up and pushed her chair in. After standing another brief moment, she decided with relief that the Grandma Cabot confrontation was over. "I'm going to my room; I want to put on some sweats and get comfortable. Then I'm going to have a snack."

She left them sitting in silence, but Mavis knew they would be banging their gums together as soon as they heard her bedroom door close. She didn't care; they were going to accept her and love her no matter what. Soon, when they saw that she kept her grades up and didn't isolate, they would forget all about her dark look. Good, she thought. The sooner, the better.

Once alone, Mavis changed her clothes and then

tore into some liver. She took note, with much disappointment, that she had only one piece left. After counting her money, she decided that she would go to the market the following day after school and reload; she would save the last piece for tomorrow.

She left her room to join her mother and grandmother when she was finished. Mavis was working her way through the adults in her life; she only really had her father left to deal with. Once that was over, it was pretty much easy going from there.

Mavis was feeling pretty darn good about herself, and she hadn't even eaten anyone lately.

∞

Surprisingly, Todd turned out to be the easiest person to deal with out of everyone.

Both Grandma Cabot and Jane were making more out of things than they were. Mavis wasn't afraid to face her dad; for one thing, she was in sweats and a sweatshirt. In all fairness, however, she had left her hair and eye makeup alone. She even added some dark red-black lipstick so he wouldn't think his wife and mother-in-law were out of their minds.

They acted like she was going to try to hide from the situation, but she had no intention of doing so. In the last half-hour before his arrival, she had to reassure them several times as she lay sprawled on the sofa surfing through television channels. Did they really think she was going to dodge her dad? They were overreacting.

When Mavis heard her father's car in the drive, she

turned the television off and sat up, moving to the end of the couch so her mother could sit if she chose. As Todd crossed the threshold of his home, the silence in the place deafened him.

He froze, his disheveled dark brown hair hanging over his eyes. As he peered over the top of his wire-rimmed glasses, he asked, "What's wrong?"

Grandma Cabot spoke up, her voice calm and even. "Oh, relax, Todd. Go ahead and get yourself settled in. No one has died or anything." She turned to Jane. "Now, you need to slow down. Nobody is going anywhere, and no one is dying."

Jane rolled her eyes at her mother and plopped down on the sofa next to Mavis.

"Well, now I can't just settle in!" Todd dropped his briefcase and coat to the floor and swung the front door closed. "I know that you women know I need to be able to adjust when I get home. I need to be able to breathe for a bit, for crying out loud!"

Grandma Cabot, Jane, and Mavis all stared at the floor in silence.

He left his things right where they lay and walked all the way into the family room. "Now, what's going on that is so important that you have to hit me with it as soon as I walk in the door?"

They all looked up at him; after a second, Jane held up her forefinger and pointed at their daughter.

"What?" Todd looked at Mavis, giving her a good scan, then looked back at his wife. He had an annoyed look on his face. "What!?"

"T-Todd, I think what Jane is pointing at is the fact that your daughter's appearance has somewhat changed... undesirable."

Her father looked her over again, then he sat down hard in Jane's rocker, banging the back of it against the wall. He let out a frustrated holler and jerked the chair away from the wall. When he had situated himself, he sat down again and took a deep breath.

"You mean to tell me that you bombarded me after work, at the front door of my home, to let me know that you two hens don't care for the color of Mavis' lipstick?"

His voice was calm but filled with disbelief. Todd looked at them both, skipping over Mavis with his eyes; he had already gotten a good look at her twice. Mavis herself sat on the sofa cross-legged and wide-eyed; her lips were pressed together to keep from smiling.

At last, his eyes rested on her. "So, I take it that you are sixteen, just acting your age. No tattoos, and no tomfoolery if we go somewhere as a family, to an important function." He looked at Jane and Marguerite again. "Wow. Haven't we all been under enough pressure? Let the girl be whoever she wants to be; she's never let us down before. Now, I'm getting something to eat."

Todd stood and went to the kitchen, and Jane jumped to her feet to follow. Mavis looked over at Grandma Cabot; the woman was looking at her with love in her eyes and smiling. Mavis smiled back.

"He was right, and we were wrong." She chuckled a

bit. "We were acting like hens. I'm sorry we didn't take the fact that you are an individual into consideration."

She stood and grabbed her jacket, which had been casually strewn over the back of Todd's recliner. "I'll go help your mother get your father fed. I know you're hungry; better come get it."

Marguerite Cabot held her hand out to her granddaughter. Mavis took it, stood, and gave the woman a hug. Together, they walked hand in hand toward the kitchen.

Mavis felt her nose twitch; her Grandma was smelling like she might make a good dessert...

CHAPTER 6

Tuesday started out normal enough, but Mavis soon discovered that it would be anything but.

Not that Mavis woke to chaos; when she opened her eyes she felt great. She had dealt with her parents, teachers, and peers regarding her new look, and had that behind her, so the apprehension and dread were as well. So, with a clear mind and chipper spirit, Mavis woke at the crack of dawn and chose her clothes and started to get ready.

She was sitting at her vanity, makeup finished, trying to do something creative with her hair. Actually, Mavis was considering adding some white tips or streaks to it; she didn't want to go with any bright neon colors. She preferred something basic yet cool and attractive. As she considered her options, her cell phone rang.

With a quick glance at the clock telling her it was still pretty early, she automatically assumed it was Kim. Maybe her best friend was sick or something, and was calling to tell her she wouldn't be walking to school with her. She stood and grabbed the cell from her bed, glancing at the screen as she sat back down; it was a number she didn't recognize at all. Mavis' brow was knit as she answered the call.

"Hello?"

There was a pause, then a slightly high-pitched male voice responded. "H-H-Hello?"

"Yes?" This had to be a wrong number. "Hello, are you there?"

She heard a muffled cough. "Y-Yes. Um, is this... M-M-Mavis?"

Who the heck was it? "Yeah, this is Mavis. Who is this?"

Another cough. "Um, Mavis, this is, uh, Carl. Um... Carl Collins. We have Social Studies together."

Mavis ran through the photo album of peers in her mind. Carl Collins... Carl Collins, hum. Her thoughts suddenly froze; was he that red-haired kid with thick glasses who always sat in the front of the class and always got into heated debates with Mr. Reiner about politics?

"Carl," she said slowly. "Yes, I know you. You sit in the front and have... conversations with the teacher."

The boy guffawed, and Mavis even thought she heard a couple of snorts. She winced and remained silent.

"Yes, yes! That's me!" He continued to chuckle slightly.

After giving him several more seconds to explain his reason for calling, Mavis got impatient with his nervous laughter and lack of words.

"Um, Carl, I'm getting ready for school." She began to drum her fingernails on the vanity top. "Did you need something?"

Yet another cough, this one more nervous-sounding than the others. "Well, I know you were dating Jeff Deason, and I hadn't had the chance to tell you how sorry I am for what happened to him." Carl coughed several times; Mavis was losing her patience. "Anyway, I was... I was wondering if you had a date for the Winter Formal." He paused, then gave a sly-sounding snicker. "I could make you forget about him... I think that is."

Now she was angry. She didn't want to be mean to the kid, but there was no way she would ever consider a date with him. Carl Collins was strange; he would sit in class and blow his nose, then stare into the tissue, inspecting his reward, for several minutes. He did this the entire period, all year around.

"How did you get my number, Carl Collins?" Mavis' voice was a bit snider than she intended it to be, but wow.

Now the kid started to stutter again. "Um... um... from your Social Media page. Um... the personal info part."

Mavis made a mental note to set her information to private as soon as she hung up. "Carl, I don't want to be rude, and I admire your courage," she lied, "but I'm still sort of in... mourning. I'm not interested in even going to the Winter Formal."

She heard him sigh loudly, the cough. "Okay, I understand. Thanks for not laughing at me; I had to really work up the nerve to even call."

Her anger faded a bit. "No problem. And Carl?"

"Yeah?"

"I'm really sorry. I hope you find a date." She hung up without giving him a chance to answer; Mavis wasn't trying to have any more conversation with him.

With a shake of her head, Mavis tossed the cell on the bed and went back to her hair. As soon as she looked in the mirror she knew what to do: she would tease it all around and make it stand up big! It would give her a pow! Sort of look, like she belonged on the cover of a compact disc or something. When she was finished, one glance told her she was right: she looked like a rock star.

She stood and gave herself a once-over in the full-length mirror that hung on her closet door. For an outfit, she had chosen black skinny jeans tucked into a little pair of pointy-toed 'witch boots' as she liked to call them. They had a short heel, but it was just as pointy as the toe. Mavis had picked them up during a summer sale at a consignment shop, and she had loved them. Unfortunately, they sat, unworn, in her closet until now; she had never had the nerve to sport them.

Her top was a long-sleeved white cotton shirt with a black t-shirt over it. The t-shirt was old and worn and used as well. It had a great big anarchy symbol on it. Her mother had only let her wear it to work in the yard, but this was a new day. Dressed, Mavis grabbed her leather jacket, computer and book bag, and cooler; she had to double back for her cell, which she slid into the bag.

After putting her things next to the front door,

Mavis went into the kitchen. Two boxes of cereal were on the table, along with milk, orange juice, and toast. She plopped down and began filling her bowl.

"You won't believe what just happened to me," she began as she prepared her food. "Some kid from school got my number off Social Media and called me to ask me out! What nerve! Ugh!"

When Jane, who was at the sink, didn't answer, Mavis looked up to see her staring at her daughter.

"What, Mom?"

Jane shook her head. "That shirt, Mavis? Really?"

She looked down, then back at her mom and grabbed the milk. "What?"

Jane groaned loudly and turned back to the sink. "I hate that shirt, Mavis."

Mavis poured her milk. "I like it. Besides, you know I'm not an anarchist, and neither is anyone at Westside High, Mother. It's just a cool shirt."

Jane groaned again, louder this time.

"So," she asked. "Who was this boy?"

Mavis chewed and swallowed some cereal. "A kid in my Social Studies class, Carl Collins. He's not really... my type." Or anyone's type, for that matter, she thought. "Anyway, he got my cell number from Social Media, which reminds me: I have to change that."

Jane turned around and took a sip of her coffee. "Are you going to go out with him?"

Mavis nearly choked on her cereal and quickly grabbed her milk to help wash it down.

"Uh, no."

Her mother took a seat across from her. "Why not?"

"Mom," she said, with a stare that spelled 'DUH,' "the boy studies his boogers every time he blows his nose. I'll pass."

Jane smiled. "I see. Well, I guess when the time is right, and you find someone who doesn't care for boogers, then you'll go out."

Mavis drank the milk out of her cereal bowl and reached for the box; she wanted another bowl. "You're funny. Ha, ha. I don't think I'm ready yet. Believe me, when I am, you'll be the first to know."

"So," Jane continued. "What you're telling me is that, if Carl Collins had been hot and popular, and never looked at his booger, you would have said yes?"

She gave her mom a smirk. "No. I don't want to date right now… at all."

"Well, I hope you change your mind before you're old and gray." Jane stood and went to refill her cup.

Mavis simply gave her a loud groan and an eye-roll, then tore into her cereal with a vengeance. She was done talking. All she wanted to do at that point was hear Kim at the door and head out.

Fortunately for her, Kim was on top of things, and within fifteen minutes Mavis was walking down the sidewalk with her friend. She hadn't even opened her mouth to tell Kim about Carl when her cell rang. She stopped and fished it out of her bag and looked at the screen. Another unfamiliar number; what the heck?

"Hello?"

Kim was watching her friend closely, her expression

clearly asking who it was. Mavis just shrugged at her. For a second, all she heard was silence.

"Hello?" she repeated.

"Oh, hey! Mavis? This is Casey Marshall, from school."

Mavis did know Casey Marshall, but not because they were good friends or anything. He was in both her German and Calculus classes, but he was best known for being on the swim team. Casey Marshall was one of the top swimmers on the team.

Mavis and Kim started to walk again. "Oh, hey, Casey. What's up?"

Casey Marshall proceeded to go into pretty much the same thing as Carl had: he got her number from her Social Media page. He was sorry to bother her. Did she have a date for the dance?

Now Mavis was a bit perturbed. The nerve of these guys! Without being mean or hurtful, she quickly shot him down, apologized, and hung up. She made sure to turn the ringer off on her phone at that point; no one else would probably call, but just in case.

"What was that all about?" Kim asked after she had dropped the phone back into her bag.

Mavis rolled her eyes and growled. She told Kim how Carl Collins had called first thing, then filled her in on Casey's call. "I don't know what's going on, but I don't want anything to do with it right now."

"Mavis, it is nearly November." Kim sounded impatient. "Maybe you should consider going to the dance. It's more than a month away; if the right boy asks, you should accept. You might be more than ready by then, and if you wait it will be too late."

Mavis stopped and turned to her friend. "Let it go. As of today, I don't want to go to the Winter Formal, got it?"

"Got it."

They continued on to school, discussing a fight Kim had with her brother Kenny the night before. It was a funny story and had Mavis laughing all the way to the school doors. It was just the emotional break she needed to face the day.

CHAPTER 7

By lunch period that day, Mavis was nearly at the end of her rope.

The calls from Carl Collins and Casey Marshall had been nothing more than the tip of the iceberg. Before she even got to second-period Science, another guy, this time a kid running for class president, asked her out as well, but not to the dance. He wanted to take her bowling that weekend; she refused.

After both second and third periods, Mavis endured two more date requests. She was ready to either punch someone or cry, and she didn't know what to do. What the heck was going on that all these boys were approaching her at once? Had her new look gone and made them think she was some kind of tramp or super-easy? All she wanted to do by the time she and Kim were on their way to the cafeteria was cry.

The two girls sat alone in a corner with their lunches, Mavis with her back to the large room, and Kim across from her, scanning all the other students. It seemed like countless boys were looking in their direction and smiling, while all the girls were pointing and smirking. Kim gave Mavis the run-down on all of it;

she simply didn't want to make eye contact with anyone.

About ten minutes before lunch was over, a boy started to approach them. When he got about four feet away, Kim held up her hand and shook her head. Mavis let her handle it.

"No, she doesn't want to go out, so don't ask," Kim said flatly. The kid walked away, head down.

After spending another minute watching Mavis stare at her empty tray, Kim had had enough. "I'll be right back."

The girl stood and crossed the cafeteria. Mavis turned slightly, keeping her back to everyone, and saw that Kim was walking toward her boyfriend, Shawn. He was seated with other members of the football team, and Mavis watched her tap his shoulder and motion for him to step away to talk to her.

The pair went off as far from other students as they could. Mavis could no longer see them, so she turned back to the table and finished her milk. She glanced at the clock; if Kim didn't hurry up, they were going to be late. Mavis began to pile garbage on her tray, and she stacked it on top of Kim's.

"Okay," her friend suddenly said from right behind her. "Let's get out of here."

In a few short minutes, they were walking up the hall heading to their next classes. "Okay," Kim began as they went. "I thought Shawn might have heard rumors or something, and I was right."

Mavis stopped dead in her tracks and turned to her friend. She glanced around at all those passing by and rolled her eyes at the looks she was getting. "What did he say?"

Kim gave a simple shrug. "All the guys think you're super-hot."

Mavis stared at her. "What?"

They started walking again. "That's it: all the guys think you look hot. There's nothing more to it, Mav."

"So, you're telling me that this crap is going on just because they think my new look is hot?" she asked.

Kim nodded. "Yep. Look, I gotta go."

They were standing in front of the band room; Kim played the flute, and that was her next class. Mavis gave her a nod and walked away, dumbfounded. She couldn't believe she was being bombarded by boys for such a dumb reason. Lots of girls were 'hot'; she never saw the boys act like this with those girls, though.

Mavis had Calculus, which was just down the hall from the music room. Just as she was approaching the door, she felt a hand on her shoulder. She turned to see a boy with longish blond hair with a goofy smile on his face. Since she didn't know him, she thought he was, more than likely, a freshman.

"Yes?" she snapped.

The kid shrugged. "Wanna go to Sports Burger with me after school?"

Mavis thought, 'What the heck?' Then she proceeded to roll her eyes and groan. This one would be harder to reject because of his age. She didn't want to hurt his feelings too badly; she knew it took some guts for the poor, pimply-faced kid to even think about asking. After she let him down easy, she quickly changed her privacy settings on her Social Media page; she didn't want any more calls once she got through all the face-to-face date requests.

Once that task was completed, Mavis couldn't get to class fast enough.

∞

By the time Mavis walked into her house that afternoon, she was exhausted by the day's events, and she was starving to boot. It was all she could do just to close the front door behind her, drop her books, and lean back against it in relief. What a day! She couldn't be happier that it was over.

"What's wrong with you?"

Mavis was leaning against the door with her eyes closed, catching her breath and calming her thoughts. At the sound of her mother's voice, she opened one eye to look at her but didn't move another muscle. Jane stood in the kitchen doorway with a cast-iron skillet in her hand and a dish towel.

Mavis groaned and closed her eyes again. "Ugh. Don't ask; you don't want to know."

Jane smiled slightly. "Don't tell me you're getting flack at school over your gorgeous, colorful new look!"

Mavis gave another groan, but this one was louder and much more dramatic. She stepped forward and picked up her cooler, which was now filled with liver again, thanks to her in-and-out, speedy trip to the market once she walked Kim home. She also grabbed up her bag and purse.

"I'm going to put these in my room," she said. "I'll be right back, and I'll tell you everything. You'll be surprised, considering your sarcastic comment, Mother."

Jane maintained her smile and went back into the kitchen, while Mavis made her way to her room, arms full and mouth grumbling. Wasn't her mother quite the comedienne, making cracks about her looks like that. Ha! Wait until she heard that Mavis' grouchy mood and exhaustion had nothing to do with being teased; quite the opposite, in fact.

She got her cooler put away, fighting the temptation to tear right into her tasty, bloody snacks. Next, Mavis decided that the best thing she could do was put on some sweats and get comfortable; she didn't plan on leaving the house for the rest of the day. Yes, it would be good to take a break from all the attention, no matter how positive it was. Her cell phone ringer was still off, and it was lying on her bed in silence; she thought she would leave it that way for a while.

But, just as she pulled her hoodie over her head, the phone light caught her eye: it was ringing, and it was another number she didn't recognize at all. She growled at her phone and snatched it up. Mavis was ready to snap.

"Hello! Who is this?"

She heard cheerful male laughter. "Hey, Mav, what's up?"

Only those close to her called her Mav, and her father and Jeff (rest his soul) were the only males to do so. Who the heck was this? No one she knew, for sure.

"Who is this!?" she repeated, much sharper this time.

The cheer and laughter disappeared immediately. "This is Colin Handley. I'm on the football team?"

Mavis did a mental head slap; another one? He must have gotten her number from Social Media before she changed her privacy settings. "Oh, hi, Colin. What's going on?" No need to be rude; he was going to ask no matter what, she knew. Mavis didn't want to add insult to her rejection, so she simply decided to let him down easy, just like the others.

"I know you had kind of a rough day today," he began. "I hope it wasn't too bad for you."

His thoughtful words took Mavis back a bit. She sighed and sat down on her bed. "I'm a survivor." She paused and tried to drum up Colin's face in her mind. "Look, Colin. I'm kind of embarrassed; I know your name, and I know you're on the team, but I can't seem to get a picture of you in my mind."

"I sit behind you in Calculus, actually," he said. "Tall, blond hair that my mother wishes I would cut. I'm the one that old Jacobi is always hacking on. We're also in Art together."

Mavis recalled him all at once. "Oh, yeah! Okay! Sorry; I've had so much going on the last couple of months."

"Um, yeah. I know." He paused. "Look, with that being said, I'm not trying to bother you. In fact, I've wanted to talk to you since last year, but... well, you know how it is. I was going to sort of try when school first started, but Jeff beat me to it." His voice sounded sort of sad. "With him being my best friend for so long, I backed off. You know how it is."

Mavis gave a sympathetic noise of agreement.

"Well, I just wanted to ask you out. You know, just maybe to hang out." He sounded nervous. "I understand if you don't want to, being so soon after... well, anyway. That's all I wanted."

Mavis realized she wasn't angry or frustrated. Maybe it was the way he talked to her like a human being before asking. Maybe it was the fact that he had been good friends with Jeff. Whatever it was, just hanging out didn't sound so bad. As long as they stayed a couple feet from each other, poor Colin would be safe. Besides, if every other boy knew she went out with someone, they would likely let her be.

"What did you have in mind?" she asked.

Colin gave a nervous chuckle. "Actually, on Sundays, I volunteer at the humane shelter. I thought maybe you would like to come and check out the animals. I get to let them out and play with them a bit, the dogs I mean. It would be cool to have someone to hang with while I do it."

Truth be told, Mavis thought it sounded like a heck of a good time. "You know, as long as it's on a friendly basis, I would like that. When?"

"Sunday morning? I could pick you up around nine?" Colin suggested. "I get done around noon."

Mavis and her family didn't leave for Grandma

Cabot's until between two-thirty and three. "That would be good," she replied. "So, I'll see you then. Oh, hey. How did you get my number?"

Colin paused. "Uh, Shawn Maher gave it to me. Don't be mad at him; I kinda nagged him."

Mavis was furious, but she said nothing.

"So, you were good friends with Jeff?" She recalled her deceased boyfriend mentioning him, but she'd never met Colin face to face.

"Yeah," he replied. "I hope he wouldn't be mad, but he knew I liked you."

"I don't think he would be," she reassured. "Besides, we're just friends, right?"

Colin chuckled. "Right. So, Sunday then?"

"Sunday."

They said their goodbyes and Mavis stared at the phone. She was going to kill Shawn. How many guys had he given her number to? She would take care of that later; for now, she needed to eat.

CHAPTER 8

"So, when do you plan on telling me about your terrible, horrible day?"

Jane sat across the kitchen table from her daughter, who was stuffing her face with pizza rolls. Jane had made an entire bag, and since Mavis had come out of her room, she had put away more than half. Her mother had given up on being shocked and amazed at her appetite weeks ago, so she just sat, coffee in hand, and waited.

Mavis swallowed her massive bite and washed it down before giving her mother a shrug. "Well, since before I left the house, all the way until just before I came out here to eat, I have been asked out by everyone from freshmen students to the Pope himself. They trolled my social page for my number, which I have now blocked, and have been calling like crazy."

Jane raised her eyebrows. "To ask for dates?"

Mavis nodded. "Not quite what you expected, I know." She popped a pizza roll into her mouth and moaned with pleasure. "But that's just part of it. I just got a call in my room from a good friend of Jeff's; I accepted his invitation to hang out on Sunday morning… just as friends."

She braced herself for her mother's reaction, which turned out to be a good idea because the woman's face not only lit up with a massive grin, she also nearly exploded with excitement.

"Are you kidding?" She leaned forward, nearly spilling her coffee. "Why this one? Why now?"

"Well," Mavis began, "for one thing, he didn't just jump right into asking me out. He asked about my day, and about all the unwanted attention I had been getting. Next, he apologized for even asking; he was Jeff's good friend, and he didn't want to jump the gun, I guess. Then, when he told me what he wanted to do when we hung out, well, I couldn't resist."

Jane waited a moment, and when Mavis didn't go into more detail, she got jumpy. "Well?"

"Jeesh, Mom." Mavis shook her head and pushed her plate away. "It seems he volunteers at the humane society; he wanted me to go with him Sunday morning for a couple of hours to play with the dogs."

"Oh, how sweet!" Jane rose to warm her coffee up. "Is he cute? What's his name?"

Mavis crossed her arms over her chest and thought about the first question. Yes, she would have to say that Colin Handley was cute; probable borderline gorgeous. She knew he had dated, and usually had girls fawning over him, but to onlookers like Mavis, he had never seemed overly interested.

"Yes. He's good-looking. His name is Colin Handley."

Jane stopped pouring, coffee pot in mid-air. "Handley… Handley. I wonder if his mother is Charlene. She volunteers with me on the senior meal delivery program. She's very pretty." She sat back down. "So, maybe you'll go to the Winter Formal after all?"

Mavis shook her head. "I told him, we are just friends. It's too soon after Jeff…" She stood up to put the small handful of leftover pizza rolls into a baggie. "That reminds me: I need to call Kim. I have a bone to pick with her."

"Well, I can't tell you how happy I am that you have a date," Jane muttered.

Mavis groaned. "We're hanging out, Mom. It's not a date!"

With the food put away and her plate in the dishwasher, Mavis went to her room and dialed Kim on her cell.

"Hello?"

Mavis cleared her throat. "Well, if it isn't Little Miss Traitor."

Kim paused. "What? Mavis, what does that mean?"

She lay back on her bed. "Well, guess who called me after I got home."

"Um, half the school?" Kim broke out into laughter.

"Funny." Mavis was not impressed or amused. "Colin Handley."

"Colin Handley called you?" Kim sounded like she was smiling; Mavis was going to kill her.

She stood from her bed and began to pace around the room. "Yeah, Colin Handley. Guess how he got my number?"

Kim didn't hesitate. "Social Media?"

"No, I fixed that little issue." Mavis paused for effect. "He got it from your goofy boyfriend, Shawn. Trust me when I say that your little love is a dead man."

She heard Kim gasp. "Shawn gave out your number?"

"Yep."

"Mavis, I can't believe it!" Her best friend actually sounded stunned. "He knows what you have been going through! He knew you don't want to date right now. Oh, I'm gonna kill him myself!"

Plopping back on the bed, Mavis replied, "Yeah, well, I did agree to hang out with the guy at his volunteer job Sunday morning, so a good tongue-lashing should be sufficient. We can probably spare Shawn's life, though."

Kim was silent for such a long time that Mavis thought she had dropped the call. "Kim?"

"I'm here." She cleared her throat. "So, you're going on a date?"

"It's not a date!" Mavis practically yelled into the phone.

Kim chuckled. "So, what is it?"

After a long sigh, Mavis replied, "We're just hanging out, no boyfriend or girlfriend stuff at all. He works at the animal shelter, so he's taking me there to play with the dogs, that's all."

"Maybe you'll go to the ball."

"I'm not!" What was it with these people? "Look,

just tell Shawn he's in the dog house. When I see him, I'm going to give him a piece of my mind, and if he gave my number to anyone else, police dogs wouldn't find his body!"

Mavis hung up before Kim could answer; it didn't matter, because she knew her friend was laughing her butt off anyway. But it didn't sound like such a bad idea, killing Shawn. Maybe if she had him for dinner, she could guarantee Colin's safety.

Funny, Mavis thought to herself. Very, very funny.

A glance at her phone told her she had missed two calls while in the kitchen. She listened to the messages to discover they were more of the same: guys wanting dates. She hoped they had gotten her number from Social Media; otherwise, Shawn was about at the end of his line. She erased the messages, made sure her ringer was off and set about doing her homework. Mavis wanted to get it done so she could go to the consignment shop and pick out some clothes to go with her new self.

Man, was she glad Tuesday was almost over.

By the time Mavis was sitting at her vanity getting ready for school on Wednesday morning, she felt that the worst of the attention she had been getting had passed.

She chose fairly conservative clothing that day but kept it all in black. Black denim, black tank, and gauzy black shirt with her leather jacket, as well as black heels, were good enough for the day. Mavis also added a bit of pale powder to her face; she had noticed that the gray streaks and veins that had been developing over her body were becoming a bit darker. It disturbed her a bit, but because she felt strong and healthy, she pushed it out of her mind. She would cope with it using makeup for the time being.

No one had tried to call her phone at all since she turned in the night before. There were no missed calls, and no messages logged, text or otherwise, and she found it to be a great relief. Yes, today would be a better day, she thought. She would be able to concentrate on her school work. Maybe she would even get a chance to say hello to Colin Handley, even if it was only in passing. Mavis expected to have fun with the animals on Sunday.

She ate a huge breakfast consisting of a massive omelet and three pancakes that were nearly as big as her plate. Mavis knew her mother rose early to feed her so well and she voiced her appreciation. She even gave Jane a big hug and sloppy kiss, which her mother hated, so she did it on purpose. She ate fast, which was a good thing, because, in no time, Kim was at the door, and they were on their way to school.

"You realize I'm going to chew out your boyfriend, don't you?" Mavis asked as they walked.

Kim groaned. "You should know, by the way, that I already did. He swears he didn't give your number to anyone else, and he won't do it again." She paused. "I really think he thought he was helping, so go easy."

Mavis thought about Kim's words. Maybe poor Shawn was sick of hearing Kim complain about Mavis not going to the Winter Formal; after all, she was sure that's just what her best friend was doing. He was probably just trying to save his own skin.

"You're sure he didn't give it to anyone else?" she asked.

Kim stopped and made Mavis look her in the eyes. "I swear." She held up her hand like she was being sworn into court to testify. "On my life, I promise. Can't you just let it go? I made him feel crappy enough, on your behalf, of course."

"Fine."

The two took off again. "So," Kim continued casually. "What is it you're always carrying around in that goofy cooler?"

The girl had never really asked before, and Mavis decided to have a little fun. "The souls of my enemies."

"Ha, ha." Kim wasn't amused. "Really, Mav. What is it?"

Mavis chuckled. "Just my snacks. If I tote them along, then I have them at school, and that keeps me from robbing the lunches of skinny boys or holding up Mrs. Beasley in the cafeteria."

Kim laughed. "Old Beasley would probably kill you and turn you into a casserole."

Mrs. Beasley had been the lunch lady for so long that Mavis thought she might have learned to cook while working for President Lincoln or something. The old woman was so grouchy that she even scared the fish sticks into submission.

As it turned out, the rest of the day did pass easily,

with minimal stress for Mavis. She wasn't asked out once, and she did get the chance to talk to Colin. She told him she was looking forward to Sunday and thanked him again for his consideration on the phone. He offered to carry her books and walk her to class, but she politely refused. Mavis told him that, if things went well, she would eagerly let him next week, and Colin Handley said he understood, but not before he took a rain check and told her he was going to hold her to it.

So far, Mavis liked him; maybe they could be good friends. All she knew was that she didn't want to ever eat anyone again, and boys seemed to be the most dangerous. With all the kissing and stuff, she didn't know if she would lose control. It was best to just keep things platonic until her weird tastes passed.

She hoped they would do just that, and soon; she wanted to get on with her life.

CHAPTER 9

When Mavis got home that afternoon, her mother announced that they would be going to Grandma Cabot's to help her move a sofa and fill her countless bird feeders. Mavis changed into something more comfortable, something she wouldn't worry about getting dirty. It was always her job to help with the bird feeders, if she happened to be there when filling time came, so she knew what she would be doing.

They set off just after four, and for the first few minutes of the drive, they were silent. Mavis stared out the window and hummed along to the radio, while Jane seemingly was concentrating on the road. But the peace in the vehicle was short-lived.

Jane suddenly reached out and turned the radio off. "So, what do you want for supper tonight?"

"Hmm," Mavis replied. "I'm not sure; what do you have in mind? I don't know what all we have."

Her mother gave a half-smile. "Well, pretty much anything you want. I did the shopping today, so we're loaded." She paused. "Oh, that reminds me: I was standing at the meat counter at the market today, and Al the butcher told me the strangest thing."

Mavis' heart immediately began to pound; she knew what was coming.

"He told me, when I went to buy liver, that they were out." Jane paused and glanced at her daughter. "They told me you had cleaned out all the liver yesterday; pork, beef, chicken… the works."

It was best to keep quiet, Mavis knew, at least for that exact moment.

Now Jane gave a laugh. "I argued with him. I mean, why would my daughter buy a ton of raw liver, and not put it in the refrigerator?" Another glance at Mavis. "Well?"

She didn't even have to think about an answer; the perfect lie rolled off her lips as easily as a stringer of drool. "I bought it and took it to the lunch ladies, so I could have it for lunch every day, that's all."

"Every single day, Mavis?"

She shrugged. "Yeah. I guess I'm kinda addicted to it. Dr. Meadows said we usually crave foods that will nourish a deficiency. I've been craving it."

Jane pulled the car into Grandma Cabot's driveway and shut off the ignition. She turned to Mavis and studied her for a long moment. For a minute, Mavis was worried her mother was going to call her on her lie, and she was nearly right.

"So, if I called the lunch lady she would tell me this is true?" The look on Jane's face was very skeptical. "I mean, I just keep thinking about the raw pork chop you stole, and the bone I caught you with. Are you sure you aren't eating it raw, Mavis?"

She made a face that was filled with false appalment. "Eewwww! That's just gross!"

The relief on Jane's face was obvious. She gave a sigh and then smiled. "Of course, it is. I feel silly. Okay, I believe you. But you should have told me. Until this craziness with your hunger passes, I will buy the liver, so you don't have to. Then you can take it to school in your snack cooler. I assume you have enough for a month?"

Mavis shook her head, ready to fib again. "No. They had only a couple slices of the pork and beef, and I got the last tub of chicken livers. It'll be gone by Monday."

Jane sat back and unlocked her seat belt. "Well, Al said they'd have stock on Friday. I'll buy you a week's worth then." She smiled and patted Mavis' shoulder. "You should have told me; there is nothing you can't tell me. Why didn't you say anything?"

Mavis undid her own belt. "Come on, Mom. All this is embarrassing enough. Well, I didn't want to add to your stress."

The two of them hugged, then made their way into her grandma's house. Mavis felt so much better about being found out regarding the liver. Now she wouldn't have to scrap and sneak to get what she desperately needed. Now she could rest assured that Colin Handley would be safe, thanks to Al the Butcher and his big mouth.

∞

Moving Grandma Cabot's sofa turned out to be just the tip of the iceberg. She was actually rearranging her entire living room. Once Mavis and her mother realized this, they knew they would be there for a while. Since the bird feeders did need filling, Jane directed Mavis to take care of the job, then come back inside and help with the rearranging, or whatever was left of it.

Grandma Cabot was a bird feeder addict. She loved to watch her fine feathered friends flit from place to place, and in an effort to lure them, the woman had posted more than thirty small feeders in various places all over her backyard. Mavis knew she would be filling them for about an hour.

She went to the shed and put in the combination on the lock. Soon, she had it opened, and she took a single ten-pound bag of seed from a stack of about fifteen bags that were neatly piled on the floor in the corner. After ripping the bag open, Mavis hauled the seed out and started to make the rounds.

For the first twenty minutes, everything was normal enough. Mavis filled and moved to the next, singing a song from the radio. The little birds didn't scatter too far when she came near; they were very used to people, thanks to her grandmother. When Mavis would approach a feeder, any little birds there would hop a couple of feet away and watch her. She would talk baby talk to them and laugh at their cute little selves.

But that all changed when she got into the far corner of the huge, fenced-in yard.

Mavis approached the largest feeder, the one her grandmother called 'The Condo.' There was only one bird there: a little sparrow. As she got closer, the little fellow hopped onto the fence but remained fearlessly about a foot away watching her as she took the feeder down and removed the lid.

Just as she bent, bag in hand, to pour the seed, Mavis smelled it.

It was a light meaty smell, sort of like raw chicken, but more earthy. She stood up and looked around, expecting to see a rabbit or squirrel, but there was nothing. Mavis bent back down to pour, and the little sparrow flapped its wings excitedly: the smell returned to her in a rush.

It was a little bird.

Immediately, Mavis seemed to lose her train of thought. She stared at the little guy and watched him as he cocked his head and chirped. A smile began to come over her face, and she didn't even consider the fact that she was thinking crazy thoughts. She was as out of her mind as she was in Jeff's car the night of homecoming… the night he had 'died.'

Keeping her eyes on the little bird, and speaking soothingly, Mavis took some of the seed into her hand. The little, tiny being cocked its head back and forth a couple of times, and hopped a couple of inches closer to her on the fence. Mavis quickly glanced toward the house; she could see her grandmother through the large picture window in the dining room; she was pointing at something and saying something to Mavis' mother.

At the exact moment that Mavis turned back to the bird, the little fellow flapped his wings and landed right in her hand. He began to peck eagerly at the seed that sat in her palm. A smile crossed Mavis' face, but it had nothing to do with the little life she was holding being cute; it was because she could eat it.

Then, something came into the very edges of her vision.

She turned her head sharply, and the little guy got startled. He quickly flew off, which would have angered Mavis if she hadn't been watching what had distracted her. Not two feet away, an ugly, dirty mole popped his head out of the ground.

The sparrow was forgotten. As quick as lightning, Mavis dropped to her knees, and in a motion so fast it could be easily missed with the naked eye, she plucked the mole out of the ground and sank her teeth into its fur-covered flesh. The thing clawed at her and fought like crazy, but only for a moment. Mavis didn't feel a single scratch or even the superficial bite the rodent delivered to her finger; she simply ripped and tore at the thing with her teeth, eating as quickly and efficiently as possible, as to not be seen or caught by her mom or her grandma.

It didn't take long. She ate as much as she could as fast as possible, then threw the warm, dripping carcass over the fence and into the alley. She was covered in blood, and as her head began to clear, she knew that her face was likely saturated as well. Mavis dragged her sleeve over her face and looked at it: yep, lots of blood, and even a bit of fur.

"Mom!" Mavis yelled hysterically and began to make her way to the house. "Mom, I have a nosebleed!"

As she neared her grandmother's residence, Mavis could see both the women cutting through the dining room, practically running as they made their way to the sliding glass door. Mavis threw her head back and held her sleeve up to her nose; it wouldn't do to fake a nosebleed if she didn't truly act like that was precisely what was going on.

The sliding door flew open. Jane took one look at her daughter and picked up her pace. "Mavis, what on Earth happened?"

"My nose is bleeding," she replied, her voice muffled by the material of her sweatshirt sleeve.

Jane dropped to her knees, and Mavis saw her grandmother run back for the house; she returned in mere seconds with a large towel in hand. Soon, Grandma Cabot was kneeling in the grass as well, pressing the towel up to Mavis' face and supporting her head as she put it back as far as it would go.

"What happened?" Jane repeated. "Did you hit your face on something?"

Mavis shook her head. "It just started bleeding." Her voice was muffled from the towel.

"Oh, my." Grandma Cabot's brow was knit severely. "I hope this isn't a sign of something really bad. I'm telling you, if that quack Dr. Meadows, misdiagnosed this girl and this is serious, you had better sue!"

"I think it's done." Mavis tried to tell them she was fine, that she thought the bleeding had stopped.

The women ignored her. "Mother, I think the doctor knows what he's talking about." She turned back to Mavis. "Do you feel okay?"

"Oh, heck! She's not going to tell you the truth!" Grandma Cabot's voice was stern. "She doesn't want to worry you!"

"Done bleeding now," Mavis insisted.

Jane growled. "My daughter would not lie to me about something like that!" She turned to Mavis. "I asked if you feel okay!"

Mavis lost her patience. She reached up and grabbed the towel, then pulled it violently from her face. "I said it's done now, and I feel fine if the two of you would listen!"

The women shut their mouths immediately, then proceeded to sit back on the grass on their rear ends. "Okay. I'm sorry." Jane looked at Grandma Cabot, who was now acting like she had nothing to do with the conversation.

"Anyway," Mavis continued, "I bumped it a couple of minutes before it started, so that was probably it. I just didn't realize it was bleeding, then when I put my hand up there, I realized it." She turned to her grandmother. "It's nothing serious, I'm fine!"

"Well!" Grandma Cabot stood up off the ground and gave Jane a gentle slap on the shoulder. "Mavis, you go get cleaned up, and leave those clothes here; I'll wash them, and you can wear one of my sweatsuits if you want. I'll go in and lay one out on my bed for you." Mavis stood, and her Grandma and Mom looked her up and down. "I think you might want to take a shower."

Ten minutes later, Mavis was standing beneath the

steaming shower spray, humming and thinking about what she had done. The mole's flesh and blood had energized and invigorated her in a way that she hadn't felt since... Jeff; she felt outstanding. Her mind was sharp, and she felt strong. The liver didn't make her feel that way; it was more like a bandage on a bullet wound, or a crappy little snack people would eat to tide them over until their next meal. Well, the liver would have to do for now; she would never get away with hunting moles all day long.

She pushed the incident out of her mind; Mavis wouldn't let such a simple thing set off her cravings. If she lost control now, it would surely spell out trouble, clearly and concisely. No, the thing with the mole had been nothing more than a slip, a fluke.

Mavis focused on forgetting it as she poured apple-scented shampoo into her hand and began to hum the tune to 'Dixie.'

R.W.K. Clark

CHAPTER 10

"Okay, class, since some of you are a bit behind on *Brother's Keeper*, I will expect two, and I said two, chapters by tomorrow, along with oral summaries." Miss Hawkins was speaking quickly, trying to beat the bell. "These summaries will be how we spend class time tomorrow, so be up to date. You know who you are!"

The bell rang, and the students all began to scramble.

"Mavis! Could I see you before you leave please?" Miss Hawkins was yelling over the voices and shuffling of her students.

Mavis jerked her head toward Miss Hawkins as she grabbed her things from beneath her desk; the teacher was motioning with her forefinger for the girl to come to the desk. Mavis sighed, grabbed her bag, and complied.

When the noise died down, Mavis asked, "You wanted to talk to me?" She glanced at the clock, not wanting to be late for her next class.

Miss Hawkins noticed. "I'll be quick; if we take too long, I'll give you a pass. Your mother called this morning."

Mavis groaned.

"She said you had a bloody nose yesterday, and with your anemia, she just wanted all of your teachers to keep an eye on you." Mavis was going to kill her mom. "Are you feeling all right?"

Mavis rolled her eyes a bit and smiled. "Yes. She's just a worrywart. I bumped my nose while helping my grandmother in the yard, and it bled a bit. I suppose it bled a lot, but it was an accident, Miss Hawkins, not a spontaneous nosebleed or anything."

"Well," the teacher continued as she walked Mavis to the door. "She loves you and is just concerned. Don't be too upset with her." She opened the door and held it to let Mavis leave, and a couple of early birds shuffled in. "And don't be surprised if other teachers ask, as well."

"I won't." Ugh! Her mother! "Thanks, Miss Hawkins."

Mavis stepped out into the hall and nearly ran headlong into Colin Handley.

"Hey, Mavis!" he said with a smile.

She immediately blushed. "Hi, Colin. I'm running a tiny bit late; sorry, I can't really talk."

She started to head to the stairs; Science was down one floor. Colin walked with her. "You have Science, right? I have History on the same floor; I'll walk with you if you don't mind."

Mavis glanced at him and smiled. "Sure."

Relief came over his face. "Good."

The two started walking, both feeling pretty shy.

After several seconds, Mavis began to feel a little uncomfortable with the silence. Her mind raced as she tried to come up with something to say.

"Um, so, how long have you volunteered at the animal shelter?"

He looked relieved again as if her question had saved them both. "Since ninth grade. I love it. My parents wanted me to get some work ethic without compromising my sports at school, so volunteering was the solution, and since I love animals it was perfect." They started down the stairs. "Now I actually have a real job. I bag groceries and stock shelves at the market on Saturday mornings and Sunday evenings. Sometimes, when I'm done with practice, I help clean up and close on the weeknights."

"Busy guy," Mavis replied as they headed up the hall to the Science lab.

When they got to the door, they stopped. "Do you work?" Colin asked.

Mavis shook her head. "No, but I will be this summer if I have my way." She jerked her head toward the classroom door. "I should go."

"Yeah," Colin said. "Me too."

She grabbed the handle to the door, then paused and turned to him. "Looking forward to Sunday."

He blushed. "Me too." Suddenly, he gave a chuckle. "I sound like a broken record. See you later, Mav."

The shortening of her name surprised her coming from him, but it sounded comfortable. She smiled as he walked up the hall, and took note that he turned back to her twice. Just as the bell rang, she rushed into the class and took her seat next to Kim.

"Where were you?" her friend whispered. "I waited at my locker!"

"Colin walked me to class," she replied. "He was waiting outside Lit; I didn't have a choice. Sorry."

Mr. Spencer, the Science teacher, banged his yardstick on his desk. "All right, people! Unless you're all talking about amphibian reproduction, I want quiet!"

The girls turned their attention to the short, balding, high-strung man and forgot about everything else. Except for Mavis, that is. Mavis' stomach was growling, and she was thinking about liver.

∞

The remainder of Mavis' Thursday went smoothly. While she saw Colin several times, including during lunch period, he kept his distance, but smiled and winked in her direction. Kim gave her plenty of ribbing and even apologized after class for cussing her out. She claimed she should have known her best friend was either with a teacher or talking to her new male friend. After all, Mavis would never intentionally stand her up.

On the way home, Kim asked her about something she had literally forgotten about: her birthday. It was now just the end of the first week of November; Mavis' birthday was on the twelfth, just four short days away.

"So," her friend said as they walked, "what did you tell your parents you wanted for your birthday?"

Mavis stopped dead in her tracks. "Oh, my! My birthday is Monday!"

Kim stopped as well and turned to her. "Duh! Are you serious?"

Mavis looked at her friend. "It hadn't even entered my mind, for real!" With a quick shrug, she started walking again, with Kim on her heels. "I haven't asked for anything, and to be honest, they haven't said a word. Wow, that's crazy."

"So, are you going to ask for something? What?" Kim gave a laugh. "If I were you I'd ask for money for clothes; you have to be running out of black."

"That's a good idea," Mavis replied, "But Grandma Cabot always gives me a hundred bucks or more, and I shop consignment. That's a lot of clothes. I think I'll just keep quiet and let them surprise me."

Now Kim stopped, and when Mavis turned to her, she saw a stupefied look on the girl's face.

"What?"

"Mavis, you have to have something in mind. After all, it's your seventeenth birthday." They started to walk yet again. "How about a car?"

"Nah. That's a lot to ask, what with all I've put them through with my health." She shook her head. "I'll think it over though. Since my birthday falls on a Monday, I'm sure we'll celebrate it on Saturday."

They got to Mavis' house and stopped at the end of the walk. "Let me know when my mom calls to invite you, whatever it is we're doing."

Kim started off. "Will do. I'll call you tonight."

"See ya."

Mavis went into her house and hollered to announce

that she was home. Jane hollered back, and Mavis went to her room to change and put her things away. By the time she went back out to the kitchen, her mother had a plate piled high with French fries and a cold glass of milk at her place.

"How was your day?" her mother asked.

Mavis plopped down and began squeezing ketchup all over the fries. "Better than it has been lately; it was good. How about you?"

Jane sat down, a cup of coffee in hand. "Fine. Do you feel okay?"

Mavis stopped mid-squeeze and looked at her, ketchup bottle in the air. "Wonderful. Which makes me wonder why all my teachers felt the need to ask, but whatever."

Jane winced. "That would be me. Sorry. I was worried." She waved it off. "Anyway, on a brighter note: you haven't mentioned your birthday or what you might want."

"That's funny," Mavis said as she closed the ketchup and set it down. "Kim brought up my birthday too. The truth of the matter is, I forgot all about it, believe it or not. So, I just thought I would let you surprise me."

Jane chuckled. "Forgetting is weird, especially for the birthday girl. But anyway, it doesn't matter, because your father and I already took care of the gift part, so what you get is what you get. We are going out to eat on Saturday night with Grandma. Make sure you ask Kim to come."

"I will after I eat." She popped a fry into her mouth.

"So, what did you get me?"

"My lips are sealed, lady." Jane stood up and poured more coffee. "When I finish this cup I'm going to Grandma's to help finish with the furniture. I figured you would want to stay home, so I'll finish the feeders for you."

Mavis thanked her around a mouthful of food, then turned her full attention on her plate. Jane putzed around a bit, then kissed her daughter on the cheek and left. Mavis enjoyed finishing her food in silence, and even enjoyed some liver while she refilled the ice in her little cooler.

Just as she was finishing up, her cell rang.

"Hey, Kim," she answered.

Kim coughed a little. "I got invited; my mom told me when I got home."

"I figured," Mavis replied. "I found out too: dinner on Saturday, and they already got my gift."

"I have to get one too," Kim said with a groan. "Don't tell me what you want; I'll wing it. I have to go… see you in the morning."

They hung up, and Mavis set about picking out her school clothes for the morning: a long, black peasant skirt, black tank, and long, ruffled cardigan with poet sleeves. It was perfect.

An hour later, she had done her homework, eaten another snack from the fridge, and put a movie on her laptop. She heard her dad come home and waited patiently watching her movie for her mother to call supper. All in all, it was the perfect evening.

Only Mavis knew that something in the back of her mind wouldn't stop thinking about the mole she ate at Grandma Cabot's.

CHAPTER 11

Friday started out pleasantly enough. Mavis woke up cheerful and ready to face the day, and she even found herself getting a bit excited to spend time with Colin on Sunday morning. As she thought about the 'appointment,' as she liked to think about it, she became more and more convinced she was taking a step in the right direction.

Everyone thought that she was avoiding boys and dating because of Jeff's death, which she was 'grieving,' and of course, that was partially true. But only she knew the whole truth: she didn't want to eat anyone else, and she didn't trust herself not to, especially after the mole incident at Grandma Cabot's. It was becoming more and more obvious to her that she had little to no control over her urge to eat living things. But she also believed that the key was to keep her distance and remain platonic with the opposite sex. After all, even though her friend Kim smelled like a loaded meat lover's pizza, she hadn't been tempted to rip her throat out, had she? Nope, not at all.

The fact was that the longer she avoided boys and dating, the odder it would become to those who really knew her, like Kim and her family. What soon-to-be seventeen-year-old girl wasn't interested in dating? Yes, accepting the appointment with Colin Handley was a good idea, not to mention the fact that he was pretty darn hot, to boot.

After changing her mind a few times, she finally chose a simple, casual outfit to wear: black leggings tucked inside her black combat boots and an oversized black sweater. Mavis teased her hair out all around her head and even added an extra coat of the super-light face powder she had been using to cover her slowly-darkening veins. She really liked the stark, almost white, appearance it gave her, and her black eye makeup just added to her new in-your-face look. A final once-over in her full-length mirror satisfied her, and she grabbed her bag, cooler, and purse and went out to have breakfast.

Mavis' mother was gone, but she had left a note. Jane had to help with a clothing drive at the homeless shelter, one of her many charitable ventures. She had left waffles, sausage, and scrambled eggs on a plate in the oven; Mavis pulled it out and was pleased to see the abundance: four waffles, eight sausage links, and a pile of scrambled eggs. Her mouth was watering so badly she could hardly pour her milk.

She sat shoveling her food in, enjoying having the morning to herself. It wasn't that she didn't love her mother, or appreciate all she did, or enjoy her company. Sometimes she just wanted time alone, just like everyone else. Lately, it had seemed to Mavis that she had been craving solitude more than usual, and the quietness of the morning, along with the awesome food, was just what she had been needing.

Suddenly, the screen on her cell lit up. She had turned off the ringer so she wouldn't forget before school, but it was sitting right next to her in case either Kim or her mother called. Mavis looked at the screen: it was Colin. Hurriedly, she swiped to answer it and raced to swallow her bite.

"Hello?" She could hear his voice before she even got it all the way to her ear.

"Good morning!" she replied cheerfully.

Colin chuckled. "You sound happy."

"Yeah." Mavis put her fork down and sat back, trying her best to ignore the food in front of her. "I'm in a good mood, so far anyway. How are you?"

"Good," he said. "Actually, I'm at school already… early practice all this week because of the game on Saturday. Do you think you'll be at the game?"

Football! Mavis had spaced off the fact that he played, and hadn't even considered that he might want her to come. She did a mental head-slap.

"Ugh! I'm sorry, I can't!" she told him. "I mean, I absolutely would, but it's my birthday on Monday, and when it falls on a weekday my parents celebrate it on the closest weekend day. In this case, Saturday evening."

"Oh! I didn't know." She could tell his wheels were turning now, and she wished she hadn't told him. What if he bought her a gift or something? Then she would feel obligated to call any time they spent together a 'date.' She should have lied.

"No biggie. Anyway, I'll see you Sunday, and in school, if you want."

"Yeah," he agreed. "Anyway, I'm sure to see you in school. So, I just thought I'd say good morning. Actually, I've been sort of… thinking about you, and I just called to let you know you were on my mind, and have a great day, Mav."

She smiled at his sweetness. "You too. We'll talk soon."

The two said their goodbyes, and Mavis tore back into her breakfast, glancing at the clock as she ate. Kim would be there in minutes; she had to hurry up. She began to race to finish the food, and soon had the task complete and her dishes in the washer. Mavis was no sooner finished than Kim rang the bell.

"So," Mavis asked her as they walked, "what are you going to get me for my birthday?"

Kim laughed. "Ha! I already got it, and wouldn't you like to know!"

"Aw, come on!" They played this game with each other on each of their birthdays, and they always ended up telling. "I would tell you! That's just cold!"

Kim stopped and took her excitedly by the arm. "Do you really want to know?" She had a mischievous grin on her face. "I can't hold it in any way!"

"Yes!"

"Okay, okay. You're gonna love it!" Kim took a deep breath. "A two-hundred dollar gift certificate from the mall!"

Mavis' mouth flew open. "Shut up!"

"Serious! I paid for it with my savings! Cool, huh?"

Excitedly, Mavis threw her laden arms around her friend, banging her in the back with her little cooler as she hugged her. "Oh, my! That's the best ever!"

They pulled apart and started walking again. "You don't get it 'til Saturday, and I expect you to remember it when my birthday comes, you little tightwad!"

"I love you, Kim. Thanks!" Mavis was super-excited. Even though she loved consignment shops, the mall was the place for clothes that fit her new style. It was an incredibly thoughtful gift. She would owe her friend, all right.

She told Kim how Colin had called and asked about the game on Saturday, then she filled her in on slipping about her birthday. "I hope he doesn't buy me anything. I mean, I barely know him."

"Well, he is trying to date you," Kim stated flatly. "Maybe a card would be all right."

Mavis shrugged. "Yeah, well, I guess I just feel like it's too soon, but I wouldn't reject a gift and hurt his feelings or anything."

Soon they arrived at Westside High. The girls made their locker trips and went their separate ways, both of them laughing and joking. Mavis was glad that the day seemed to be going so… normally. She was tired of trying so hard to make things appear that way.

It would be a good day.

∞

For her first two classes, and part of her third, the day went exactly as she hoped.

Mavis endured the two-chapter summaries the class had to give in Literature on *Brother's Keeper*. She was well past the other kids in the book, but she had to flip back and review each chapter briefly just to give a proper summary. When she was finished delivering hers at the front of the class, Miss Hawkins was beaming.

"Beautiful job, Mavis," the teacher told her. "I'm sure you are on schedule, and I'm sorry for those of you who have had to endure this tedious assignment. Next!"

Second period Science consisted of nothing but taking notes on amphibians and a long, drawn-out lecture at the end from Mr. Spencer on how the midterms would focus almost wholly on reproductive practices of all cold-blooded species. He also let them know they would be reviewing their segment on plant life in depth in the test as well.

Fourth period Art was Mavis' favorite subject. She had been toying with the idea of working with children when she grew up, and she had been entertaining this idea for a couple of years. But she knew, however, that if she ever changed her mind, it would be for the sake of art; she loved it, and having a career in art would be like a dream come true for her.

The class started out as usual. They were working on drawing and shading with dots or stippling. Mavis had a good start on her project, which was to be a portrait of Mother Teresa; she loved all the lines in the woman's face, and Mavis thought she was beautiful.

About halfway through the class, however, one of the student hall monitors entered the room. Mavis barely took note of him, only looking up to see who came in. She went back to work, but seconds later Mrs. Campbell called her name.

"Mavis, would you come up here for a second?"

Mavis knit her brow and nodded as she rose from her workstation. Was something wrong with her parents or grandmother? Had she left something on at home, and the house burned down? Oh, were the police there to question her some more about Jeff's death?

She walked to the front of the room and leaned over Mrs. Campbell's desk. "Yes?"

The art teacher gave her a smile. "Mr. Eagan here was sent by Principal Pearson; it seems he would like to have a word with you in his office."

Mavis looked up at the eleventh-grader who helped monitor the halls and raised an eyebrow. The kid sniffed and put his nose in the air, his thick glasses sliding back into place hard enough to make him wince. What was this about? Well, this kid wouldn't know; he was just a gopher.

"Sure," she replied pleasantly. "I'll be back."

She left the room with the monitor, who walked in front of her all the way to the stairs and then to the principal's office. Mavis didn't even try to talk to him, and he didn't say a word. All he did was give a snobbish sniff now and then, acting as though he were better than she because of his position of trust.

Nicholas Eagan stopped outside the office door, nodded once, and turned and walked away, his ticket book in hand. Off to bust more unruly students, Mavis thought with a smile. She opened the office door and stepped inside.

Mavis glanced around quickly. One girl with a snotty nose and an eyebrow piercing was sitting on the 'in trouble' bench, but other than her and the office staff, the room was clear. She approached the long main counter and smiled.

"Mrs. Benson? Nick Eagan said Mr. Pearson wants to see me?"

Mrs. Benson looked up at her, then turned and looked at the other ladies working behind her. They all gave sideways glances and pretended to be hard at work. What the heck was going on? What was this about?

"Yes, Miss Harvey," Mrs. Benson said in a snide tone. "He's waiting for you."

Mavis gave her a look of confusion. "Thanks."

She crossed the room to the principal's office door and rapped on it.

"Come in!" Mr. Pearson's voice boomed through the door.

Mavis turned the knob and stepped inside, closing the door behind her. "You wanted to see me?"

The man looked up at her and gestured toward the chairs across from his desk. "Sit down, please."

Mavis sat and waited as he finished with his paperwork. After several moments the man plopped his pen down and laced his fingers behind his head and leaned back. He studied her for several seconds; it made her feel very uncomfortable, and Mavis wanted to crawl under his desk and hide.

"So, how is your day?" he asked in a flat tone, his face free of cheer.

Mavis shrugged. "Very good, actually. Yours?"

Mr. Pearson snorted. "As good as could be expected. So, have you heard what happened in the last hour? Right here on the first floor?"

Mavis shook her head.

The man stood and began to pace around the office. "Well, we had a bit of an adventure. One of the students was reported to me as selling drugs here in school. I was forced to call the police, and they brought a dog and searched his locker. The boy was caught with a small amount of an illegal substance and arrested." He stopped in front of his desk and sat on the edge of it, looking down at Mavis with unsmiling eyes. "His locker was right next to yours, and as it turned out, the dogs went crazy when they started whiffing at your locker as well. Would you like to tell me what I found inside?"

Mavis' heart began to pound. "Well, I know it wasn't illegal substances." She gave a smile and chuckle.

Mr. Pearson laughed loudly for too long. "Oh, no. No drugs there! Nothing illegal in Mavis Harvey's locker at all!" The man chuckled as well, then he crossed around to his chair again and sat down hard. Reaching over to the floor next to him, the man lifted her little cooler and held it up in mid-air. "Would you like to explain why you have six pounds of raw liver, of various varieties, in a cooler in your locker, Miss Harvey? Not that I'm concerned that it will kill your brain cells or ruin your life, but it sure did set the police dogs off, and that interfered a bit with what the police were here to do."

Mavis felt the blood creeping up into her cheeks, and her mind was racing for an answer; fortunately, it didn't take her long to come up with one. "I'm really sorry for the problem, Mr. Pearson. Um, my mother had to volunteer at the homeless shelter today, and she didn't have time to go to the grocery store." Mavis fidgeted a bit as she lied to her principal's face. "We're having dinner with some of my parents' friends, and my dad needed bait for fishing, so my mom had me go to the market before school."

Mr. Pearson raised an eyebrow at her response. "The liver is for dinner? At your home? And you brought it to school?"

Mavis shrugged and laughed nervously again. "Well, I didn't have time to get it back home without being late to first period, so Mom gave me the cooler and ice, and she told me to bring it directly home after school so she could prepare the meal."

The man's face relaxed, and Mavis knew he believed her. It seemed she was going to be in the clear once again. What the heck were the chances that police dogs would come and smell her little meaty secret? Man, it was a good thing she was a quick thinker.

"Well," Mr. Pearson said with a smile as he stood from his chair, "I should have known you had an explanation. I have to admit, I was a bit concerned that, with your anemia and all, that maybe you were… eating it! Bahahahaha!"

Mavis joined him in his loud, obnoxious laughter, but she was mentally slapping her own forehead. How many times could she come so close to being called out on her weird cravings without them catching her red-handed and locking her up for good? Best to laugh with him.

Mavis stood as well, and Mr. Pearson handed her the little cooler, then gave her a pat on the back. "I don't think it would hurt anyone keeping it in your locker, but just to be safe, let's leave the cooler up here with Mrs. Benson, and you can pick it up before you leave for the day. For future reference, you and Mrs. Harvey should plan your shopping trips a little better."

The two left his office, stopping at the desk to leave the liver, and to explain to Mrs. Benson that Mavis would pick it up at the end of the day. She gave another apology and left the office feeling like she had seriously just dodged a bullet. Now what? If she brought the cooler to school again, and either Mr. Pearson or one of the office ladies noticed, she would be put through the wringer! Mavis was going to have to come up with a new idea, and she was going to have to make sure it was a lot more inconspicuous.

She headed back to art class, groaning. Now what? What was she going to do about bringing her delicious snacks to school?

CHAPTER 12

Mavis managed to dodge all of Kim's goofy questions when she picked up her cooler from the office after school. She simply told the same offbeat story to her best friend that she had told Mr. Pearson, and while Kim wasn't quite buying it, she did manage to give up when Mavis continued to insist that it was true. Finally, the girl changed the subject, much to Mavis' relief, and the subject was changed to the birthday dinner coming up the following night.

"So, do you have any guesses what your parents might have gotten for you?" Kim asked.

Mavis shook her head. "No, and it's funny because I haven't really thought about it. If they stay true to form, I would guess a new laptop or tablet or phone, but all three of mine were bought in the last year, and I never even really use the tablet, except on vacations." She paused, thinking. "I hope they didn't get me clothes for my new look, considering what you got me."

"Nah," Kim replied. "Before I got it, I called your mom and asked if they were getting you clothes; she said no, and my gift was perfect. What else could it be?"

"Well, Grandma Cabot always gives me money, so

they never do." Mavis was really beginning to wonder now. "You know, now that we're talking about it, I have no idea what it could be. Now you've got my head really thinking. Thanks!"

They got to the end of Mavis' sidewalk. "No problem," Kim laughed. "Well, I'd come in for a few, but I've really got to hit my homework hard. I made a stupid comment to Mr. Jacobi in Calc, and he slammed me with an extra assignment. I'll probably call if I need help."

"What did you say to him?" Mavis asked with a smile.

Kim rolled her eyes. "I told him he wasn't a fraction as good at teaching calculus as he was at decimals."

"Oh, a bad one, Kim. Terrible."

Kim shrugged and smiled. "The rest of the class thought it was hilarious. I was lucky I didn't get detention." She began to walk away, waving over her shoulder. "Talk to you later."

"Later."

Mavis noticed her mother still wasn't home; the car was gone, and Jane used the garage only in the winter. Perfect! She would grab a snack from the fridge and lock herself in her room with her laptop. It was time to do some research and find some way to keep her liver cool without a cooler. There had to be some kind of gadget!

She took her things to her room and went to the fridge, where she found two leftover pieces of fried chicken and some mashed potatoes. Mavis heated them in the oven, poured some milk, and took the food to her room. After a quick change into something comfortable, she sat on her bed, laptop open, with the plate in her lap so she could eat while she searched.

Mavis didn't have to look for long; she almost immediately wound up finding a cooler with a shoulder strap that looked more like a purse than anything. It came in multiple colors, including black, and would hold enough liver for a day. She could leave her little cooler in her closet, tucked away safely, and she could have what she needed without any suspicion. The best part was that she wouldn't have to leave it in her locker, where drug dogs or any other nosy people could find it. Now, she could carry it to class, ice, liver, and all, and no one would be the wiser; it wasn't boxy at all, just a little thicker on the bottom, flatter on the top, and closed with a Velcro flap. The bag would even keep the meat fresh for ten hours! It was perfect.

She fished out of her purse her prepaid debit card that her parents had given her for emergencies and ordered a black one right then and there. She even paid extra for next-day shipping so she would be home when it came. The cost for the bag was only twenty-dollars, but next-day shipping was an additional thirty-five. But Mavis wasn't worried as she placed the order. She would reload the money to the prepaid card with whatever cash she got for her birthday, quick and easy. If her parents were home when the cooler was delivered, she would tell them she used the emergencies only card and would explain that she would replace the money right away.

With that out of the way, Mavis cleaned her plate like a savage, chomping and snorting as she ate, oblivious to her own appearance or sounds. When the food was gone, she hit the books. She didn't have much homework, and she never did. Mavis had always taken advantage of free time in class when it came to completing her assignments, not to mention she had study hall instead of H&H on Tuesdays and Thursdays. She always used that time wisely as well.

Mavis heard both of her parents arrive home, one right after the other, just after five thirty. Jane yelled down the hall to make sure she was home, and after acknowledging her, Mavis began to pack up her books; even though it was the weekend, she had always hated senseless clutter. Just as she was ready to leave her room and join her family, her cell rang.

"Hey, Kim," she answered.

Her friend began to rattle right away. "Just wanted to let you know that I did the Calculus on my own. Pretty sure I aced it! Cool, huh?"

"Yeah!" Mavis replied, relieved that she didn't have to help. Kim had always loathed math of any kind. "Do you want me to check it? You know, just to be sure?"

Kim thought about it. "That might be a good idea. Should I stop by after dinner for a bit?"

"About seven," Mavis replied. "Is that cool?"

"See you then!" Kim hung up before Mavis could reply.

She sat there, staring at her phone, smiling and

shaking her head. "The girl is a wingnut," Mavis muttered.

Dinner consisted of meatloaf, scalloped potatoes, and corn, all of which was to die for. While they ate, Mavis decided to tell them about her purchase. They didn't care in the slightest, but let her know clearly that she was to replace it. Todd did ask her why she couldn't wait until after her birthday when she had the money, and Mavis managed to appease him by telling him she would have had to use the card to order anyway. Her answer satisfied him.

Kim showed up right before seven, just as Mavis was finishing up with cleaning the kitchen for her mother. The two girls went to her room, and Mavis proceeded to double-check her best friend's calculus. Kim lay on the floor with her feet on the wall, singing a pop song, while Mavis scanned her work.

When she was finished, Mavis took a deep breath and said, "Good thing you had me do this."

"Why?" Kim asked as she traced dance steps on the wall with her stocking feet.

Mavis snorted. "You only got one out of fifteen right, and the work on that correct one is wrong. You only got that one on a fluke, I'm afraid. You'd better get your butt up here to fix these, or you'll be spending the night."

Kim rolled over and smiled. "I should anyway."

"What?"

Kim shrugged, her smile growing. "Spend the night."

The suggestion made Mavis pause. How would she eat her nightly liver? She would have to sneak some into the bathroom somehow. Maybe when Kim showered, which she usually did when she stayed. Ugh!

"I guess," she said. "You'll have to borrow jammies."

"And call my mom." Kim jumped up and dug her cell out of her back pocket and started to call.

While Kim made her call, Mavis went out to let her own mother know. Kim was pretty much a permanent fixture around the Harvey home, just as Mavis was at the Coleman residence. The girls really never asked to stay at each other's houses; they just told their parents what was going on.

Within an hour, Mavis and Kim had the futon in Mavis' bedroom all set up and made for sleeping. Kim borrowed a pair of yoga pants and a big t-shirt, then disappeared into the bathroom for a shower. Mavis took advantage of the alone time and managed to get a nice big chunk of liver devoured before her friend's return.

Mavis showered as well, and then the two girls turned on music videos, and Jane brought them sodas and a heaping bowl of butter and white cheddar popcorn. They sat in beanbag chairs and gabbed while they fed their faces, making fun of people on the television and singing along to the music.

After a while, Mavis got quiet, and Kim noticed right away. "What's up, girl?" she asked.

Mavis shrugged. "I don't know. I had a weird dream last night, and it's kind of had me thinking, that's all."

Kim forced a handful of popcorn into her mouth and spoke around it. "What about?"

After a drink of soda, Mavis replied, "I was kind of sick or something, and I didn't want to eat anything but people. Weird, huh? It was like nothing was really good to eat but other humans."

"That is weird," Kim agreed. "It's likely you had that dream because of your low iron or something."

Mavis wanted to talk to Kim about this issue for a while, but she knew her friend's reaction to the truth would be less than pleasant. Making up some odd story was all she could come up with.

"Yeah, my iron. But Kim, what would you do if that ever happened to you? I mean, for real? And, like, no food made you feel better except bloody, raw meat? Wouldn't that be crazy?"

Kim thought about it. "I guess I would, like, go rob the morgue or something. It's not like I'd be able to just eat people whenever the urge struck me, you know?"

"Right," Mavis muttered.

She let the subject drop, but her mind was on Kim's response about the morgue. Maybe that was a solution. Maybe she should be trying to rob the morgue once a week. But then, what the heck would she do with the body? She didn't even have a car or anything to haul it with if she did do it.

Mavis pushed the issue out of her mind. It wasn't ever going to be a topic she could discuss with anyone unless she wanted to wind up in a rubber room somewhere. No, she would have to figure things out for herself, and she was going to have to keep her secret locked safely inside her own heart and mind.

At least for the time being, she was still holding on to the hope that the issue would disappear on its own. She would simply bide her time and use the solutions she had been using. That would have to be the way it would go.

But for now, Mavis had to deal with the fact that her freshly-showered best friend smelled like a wonderful meaty pork steak.

CHAPTER 13

Mavis woke on Saturday morning to a pop song blaring from her television. She lifted her head and glanced around the room; Kim was nowhere in sight. With a long groan, Mavis swung her legs to the floor and gave a stretch.

Her bedroom door flew open and Kim be-bopped in, still in her jammies. "Hey, sleepyhead! Morning!"

"Ugh!" Mavis watched as her friend grabbed the remote from the floor and began to flip through the music channels. She had just passed one playing loud, hard, heavy metal when Mavis spoke up.

"Go back! That sounded good."

Kim looked at her and flipped the channel back. An old-school video with some guy with long hair and eyeliner appeared; he was screaming about going off the rails on a crazy train.

"This?" Kim scrunched her nose up.

Mavis nodded. "Yeah."

Her friend looked back at the television. "Who the heck listens to this stuff?"

Mavis shrugged and smiled. "I don't know, but it's good. It's better than all that other crap we listen to."

Kim stared at her for a minute, then tossed the remote to her; it landed on the floor at her feet. "I'm going back out with Jane; this is awful." She started out, then stopped and turned around. "Will you lend me some clothes?"

Mavis raised her eyebrows in confirmation; her head was too busy bobbing up and down to the music. Kim shook her head and left the room, closing the door behind her. Mavis didn't even notice she was gone.

After a bit, she turned down the music and quickly ran a brush through her hair. She added a little powder to her face, just for the sake of covering her grayish veins, but she left her pajamas on. It seemed like the perfect day to be lazy.

As soon as she opened her bedroom door, Mavis smelled bacon, and her stomach screamed at her for satisfaction. She patted it and smiled. Baby's hungry, she thought. It made her almost laugh out loud.

"Mornin'!" she exclaimed as she turned and walked into the kitchen. "It smells amazing in here!"

Jane smiled at her. "Good morning, beautiful! Big day ahead! Do you want pancakes, waffles, or toast?"

"Pancakes!" Mavis sat down next to Kim at the table and poured a glass of orange juice. After a moment, Jane joined them with her coffee.

"Oh, before I forget: that boy Colin called," Jane said nonchalantly. "He said he tried to call your cell, but didn't get an answer, and he has to work today. He wants to bring your birthday gift before he goes in at eleven."

Mavis threw her head back and growled. "Aargh! I'd hoped he hadn't done that!" A glance at the clock told her it was ten. "I'd better dig in; I still have to get dressed!"

The girls hurried and ate, then went to Mavis' room to change. They were just finishing up when the doorbell rang. She went to leave the room, then turned to make sure Kim was behind her. The girl was sitting on the bed shaking her head at some video by a heavy metal band.

"This is so… headache-inducing," she mumbled.

Mavis rolled her eyes. "Turn it off and come on; if I have to do this, and you're here, you're doing it too."

"Yeah, yeah." Kim turned the set off and followed Mavis out.

Just as the girls were walking up the hall, Jane yelled, "Mavis! You have company!"

They walked into the living room to see Colin Handley sitting on the sofa with a small gift bag in his hand. He turned to Mavis and smiled, quickly rising to his feet. Kim snickered and made her way to Todd's recliner so she could sit back and enjoy the show.

"Good morning," he said. "Um, sorry to just stop by and all. I only have a couple of minutes, because I have to work. Anyway, happy birthday, Mavis!" Colin held out the pretty silver bag. "It's not much. I hope you like it, though."

Mavis reached inside the bag and pulled out a compact disc. She looked at the cover; it was a new band, and they obviously played hard rock. Mavis smiled up at Colin.

"Thank you!"

He shrugged shyly. "I don't know what kind of music you like, but I kind of assumed..." He watched as Mavis turned the disc over to read the back. "Anyway, I love these guys; they're the biggest thing in thrash right now."

"I love it! Thank you!" Mavis stepped forward and planted a quick kiss on his cheek; he smelled like freshly ground hamburger. She had to step back quickly. "I'll listen to it today."

Colin's hand went to his cheek, and his smile grew. "Well, I'd better go. Thanks for your hospitality, Mrs. Harvey." He turned back to Mavis. "So, I'll pick you up in the morning at nine?"

"Nine," she said. "Thanks again, Colin."

Mavis walked him to his car, and as he drove away she thought; man, I'm gonna have to keep my distance.

She walked back into the house to see her best friend and mother grinning stupidly.

"He's cute," Jane offered; Kim broke out in juvenile giggles.

Mavis gave a disgusted wave of her hand. "Whatever, morons."

Both of them broke out in giggles.

"Kim, don't you need to, like, go home?" Mavis really didn't want to get rid of her, but she wasn't going to be teased about such an innocent gift. "I mean, like, to help your mom, or get ready for dinner tonight?"

Kim looked at the clock on the mantel. "Okay, I'm

out of here. I do have to help in the yard." The girl opened the front door, then turned around. "What time should I be here for dinner, Jane?"

"Oh, six-thirty-ish."

"Okay," Kim responded. She looked at Mavis and made a sappy, love-struck face. "See you later, lover girl." She followed up the statement by kissing the air several times.

"Go!" Mavis practically chased her friend out the door.

When Kim was gone, she turned to her mother. "Don't you say a word, Mom!"

Jane pretended to lock her mouth and threw the imaginary key over her shoulder.

"Yeah, right." Mavis scowled.

After lunch, Todd and Jane left, saying they had to run some errands. Mavis thought she would use her free time alone to listen to her new CD, and maybe even take a nap. It would be good to spend some time thinking about how to keep her distance from Colin the Hamburger Boy during their date the following day.

∞

"Happy Birthday, dear Mavis! Happy Birthday to you!" voices rang out around her.

Every single customer in Gator's Steak House broke into applause, and Mavis blushed deeply. She couldn't help but smile, so she made it a point to focus on blowing out the candles. Soon, another round of applause broke out.

"Okay, now," Grandma Cabot began. "It's time for

the speech!"

"Speech, speech!" her parents and Kim yelled.

Mavis shrugged. "I really don't have a speech or any wisdom; I'm only seventeen. But thank you all for thinking of me and treating me so special today. I love you!"

Jane leaned forward. "Mom," she said to Grandma Cabot, "you go first."

Grandma Cabot dug in her suitcase of a purse and pulled out a card. She handed it to Mavis and planted a wet, hot-pink kiss on her cheek. "Happy birthday, love!"

Mavis opened the card, taking time to read it carefully and not appear too anxious. It turned out to be a funny card, and everyone laughed. Her grandmother had tucked a crisp new hundred-dollar bill inside.

Mavis kissed Marguerite Cabot's cheek. "Thank you, Grandma. I love you."

"Kim's turn!" Jane was more excited than Mavis.

Kim grinned at her friend and handed her another card. "Here you go, Goon. Happy crappy birthday."

Mavis stuck her tongue out and opened the card. This one was a bit more serious, talking about best friends being sisters. Inside was her gift certificate to the mall, which she waved around. She finished with that gift by giving her friend a huge hug.

"Love ya, Mav," Kim said, her eyes misting up.

"Okay!" Jane exclaimed. "Now it's my and Daddy's turn!" Both of her parents were grinning from ear to ear, and they looked as if they might jump right out of their chairs. Jane held up a little red box with a white bow. The box was tiny, so Mavis knew it had to be jewelry. She took the box, then the card her dad held.

After reading the card out loud, Mavis jumped up and hugged and kissed both her parents. It was a super-sappy card, and it almost made her cry. They rushed her through the hugs.

"Now open it!" Jane exclaimed. "Open the box!"

Mavis sat back down in her chair and picked up the small, perfectly wrapped box. She lifted it to her ear and shook it, but the sound was muffled. Her mother must have put cotton inside to protect it from her traditional shake.

Jane growled. "Open it, already!"

Mavis grinned mischievously; her mother was really wound. When she did begin to unwrap the gift, she moved at a snail's pace, removing the bow at about a tenth of a mile per hour. Jane was ready to explode.

"Just kidding, Mom."

Mavis proceeded to tear into the wee package for her mother's benefit. She stopped only to shake it once more before opening the white box, then lifted the lid. A square of cotton flew out and fluttered to the floor, forgotten.

There, nestled snuggly in more cotton, was a remote key fob with a single key on it.

Mavis looked up in disbelief. "Did you get me a car?"

Jane exploded in both laughter and applause, as did everyone else at the table. Todd jumped up and held out his hand. Mavis stared at it stupidly for a moment.

"Come on!" he exclaimed. "It's outside! That's why I drove myself and met you guys here; I had to bring the car!"

The fact that her parents had gotten her a car suddenly hit her. "Oh, my! A car?" She looked at Kim. "A car!"

Mavis grabbed her best friend's hand and practically dragged her to the parking lot as her father led the way. There, across the lot, was a small, white, two-door vehicle with a convertible top. It was beautiful!

Todd turned to her and plucked the key from the box. Using the remote, he unlocked the doors. The car honked once, the lights flashed, and Mavis could hear the locks flip.

"It's a convertible," he said excitedly. "Brand new. Now you can get that summer job next year! And you can drive to school, shop, or do whatever you want! Of course, you'll have to pay for gas with your allowance, but I plan to give you a bit of a raise to cover costs."

Mavis flung herself at her father and gave him a huge hug. "Thank you, Daddy! Thank you, thank you, thank you!"

She let go of him and turned to see her mother and grandmother standing behind them, beaming. Jane was taking pictures with her cell phone. Grandma Cabot was crying.

"Well?" Todd held his hands up, palms up. "Are you going to take it for a spin?"

"Yeah!" the girls both screamed together.

"Then we'll see you at home," he said. "Be careful!"

Mavis' parents watched as the girls jumped into the car and started it up. They waved them off and watched them drive away. For both Mavis and Kim, the adults were forgotten. As they pulled out of the Gator's Steak House parking lot, both of them gave loud hoots.

"Is this the best gift ever, or what?" Kim yelled.

"Heck, yeah!" Mavis laughed.

CHAPTER 14

Mavis and Kim ended up cruising around Greenville for the next two hours. They stopped and had ice cream, then drove up and down the main strip, honking and yelling at everyone they came across. It was sheer bliss. Mavis called her mother twice to let her know they were okay.

Kim was planning to spend the night again, so at ten-thirty the girls pulled the new car into the Harvey driveway, then stood outside in the crisp night air to admire it for about twenty minutes.

"This is going to change our entire lives!" Kim said.

Mavis laughed. "You're telling me! This spells out one thing: freedom! We can pretty much do what we want!"

They squealed and embraced each other, jumping up and down in the air. A new car was a dream come true for anyone, much less a seventeen-year-old girl and her best friend. They couldn't wait to break it in and made plans to hit the road right after Mavis got back from her appointment with Colin the following day. They would have a few good hours before dinner at Grandma Cabot's house.

"So, do you love it?" Jane was waiting anxiously for them in the house; Todd was sawing logs in his recliner.

In response, the girls began to jump and squeal again, this time with Jane joining in. Todd stirred in his chair, then grumbled a bit. They tried to settle down quickly.

"What the heck?" He sat up and ran his hand through his hair. "I take it you like it? Well, good. Now I'm going to bed." Todd stood up and gave Mavis a hug and kiss, kissed his wife, and very nearly kissed Kim, who looked like she was going to have a heart attack when he tried. "Sorry," Todd mumbled, backing away. "I'm too tired for this."

The girls stayed up with Jane until nearly one in the morning, doing nothing but eating and talking girl talk. It was wonderful, and Mavis couldn't have been happier. She admitted to her mom and Kim that it had been the best birthday she ever had.

Jane finally went to bed, and Mavis and Kim ended up passing out beneath a heap of blankets on the living room floor. It was the perfect end to the perfect day.

Even though Mavis was having another dream…

∞

She was sitting alone in Sports Burger. Colin was going to meet her there, and they were going to have lunch. He had just called her phone to tell her he was going to be a little late, so Mavis had just ordered the Monstrosity Burger with extra everything.

While she waited for Colin, and her food, Mavis looked around the restaurant at the other customers.

One little boy sat at a corner table with his mother. He wore a cowboy hat and had a long piece of straw dangling from his mouth. As he kicked his short little legs, he looked over at Mavis and smiled. "You are what you eat!" he said with a snicker. "What you eat, what you eat… you are what you eat!"

"Off with his head!" Mavis jumped and quickly turned toward the voice. A little girl in a princess costume was waving a wand in Mavis' face; she had blood smeared all around her mouth, and Mavis could have sworn there was a shred of flesh between her teeth. A woman rushed over, smiling, and grabbed the little girl up.

"Forgive my daughter," she said with a nervous laugh. "She just hates it when her food stares back at her."

The child hit Mavis on the head with her wand. "No looking! Off with his head!"

The waiter was approaching Mavis' table with a plate in his hands. She could see the top of the massive sandwich, and beside it was a large pile of fries. Fries were falling to the floor as the kid approached.

"Off with his head!"

"You are what you eat!"

The two children were still yelling their enigmatic comments; their voices grew progressively louder until they were yelling over each other. Between each of their statements, they emitted insane laughter, over and over, like a broken record.

The waiter stopped at her table and gave her a huge

smile; several of his teeth were missing, leaving gaping black holes in his mouth. One eye was popping slightly out of his skull, its milky white surface giving away its inability to see. His skin was gray and patchy, and he was missing some chunks of it here and there.

"Here you go, miss," he said in a rough, gravelly voice as a cockroach crawled out of his mouth. "The 'Colin Burger,' extra-rare!"

He set the plate down in front of her; Mavis looked it over timidly. "The 'Colin Burger'? I ordered the Monstrosity!"

The waiter began to laugh loudly, pausing only long enough to say, "Oh, this is a monstrosity!"

The entire restaurant began to roar with laughter, and the two little kids could still be heard shouting their confusing words, over and over. Now, their voices were high-pitched and squeaky. Mavis pushed the sounds of chaos from her head and studied her plate; all looked fairly normal.

Slowly, she reached out and lifted the top bun off the sandwich. Colin smiled up at her, his face a thick, half-pound patty smeared with ketchup and mustard, his hair nothing more than lettuce poking out around the top. Mavis froze, petrified with both fear and disgust.

"Oh, Mav," Colin said pleasantly. "Don't worry: I'm full of vitamins and minerals. Once they took off my head, it was easy. So, eat your fill! You are what you eat! You are what you eat!" echoed around her.

Mavis screamed and stood up. Everyone was laughing at her hysterically; everyone except the Colin

Burger, that is. His eyes were rolling around as he continued to scream the terrible words that Mavis was what she ate, was what she ate.

She ran, and just as she reached the door, the little cowpoke with the big mouth stuck out his foot, tripped her, and she hit the floor hard…

∞

Something was on top of her, something heavy and hard.

Mavis fought and kicked, screaming at the top of her lungs for someone, anyone, to help her. All of a sudden, she could hear voices. At first, they were not recognizable, but as her daze cleared, she realized it was the voice of her friend, Kim.

"Jane, help! Mavis is trapped!"

She continued to struggle as footsteps raced in her direction. "Oh, how did this happen?"

Suddenly, light flooded the room. The weight was gone, and Mavis was free. She could feel tears on her face as she gasped for breath and tried to calm down.

"Honey, are you okay?" It was her mother, stroking her hair and speaking in a soothing voice. "What happened?"

Kim answered the question that Mavis could not. "We were just sleeping. All of a sudden she started screaming, and when I woke up all the way, I could see that she had the bookcase on top of her."

Mavis struggled to sit up and look around. Books were everywhere, all over the large pallet which she and Kim had been sleeping on in the living room. With a quick glance behind her, she saw the small bookcase, which had been sitting upright and full of books at her head when she fell asleep. It was now empty and sitting askew, right where her mother left it when she lifted it off her screaming daughter.

"Oh, my, Mavis, did you have a nightmare or something?" Jane was fretting.

Mavis looked at the clock on the mantel: it was just six in the morning. She had managed to cause quite an early morning stir at the Harvey house. She shook her head and tried to clear the cobwebs and recall her dream.

It was coming back to her. "No, no nightmare," she muttered as she got closer to reality. The dream had been horrible and confusing; she would admit to nothing. "No. I must have just been sleeping rough. Wow; I knocked over the bookcase."

Jane laughed nervously. "Right on top of your head!"

Kim was stacking books and trying to get them out of the way. "I didn't even feel or hear the thing come down. Wow, Mav. I can't believe you didn't bust your head open or something."

What day was it? Mavis felt extremely disoriented and foggy, and she was finding it difficult to come back to reality. Now the dream was clear in her mind; it was almost just like the one she had about Jeff Deason when she ate him at the family picnic, and she had ended up eating him in real life! Was her dream trying to tell her she was going to do it again, only this time to Colin

Handley?

No! Mavis was in control! She would determine who she would eat and when she would eat them. She quickly shook her head, hard. What the heck was she thinking? She must not be all the way awake yet.

Mavis was aware of her mother and Kim staring at her; she must have looked crazy, shaking her head like that. "Sorry," she said with a slight smile. "I'm trying to wake up."

Jane studied her for a moment longer. "Well, I guess I'll put breakfast on. No sense in going back to bed, not if you're seeing Colin at nine. When you get your head on straight, please pick up the books and straighten up. How about the works for breakfast, girls?"

Mavis thought It's Sunday!

"Yeah!" Kim exclaimed, jumping up. "Can I get in the shower first?"

Jane was already in the kitchen. Mavis looked up at her and smiled. "Sure. Go ahead."

When Kim had disappeared down the hall, Mavis looked over the book mess. Slowly, she started to pick them all up, and after putting the bookcase back into position, she started loading them onto the shelves. Her heart was just a tiny bit heavy.

"Jeesh," she muttered as she worked. "I need to figure something out. This crap is ridiculous."

R.W.K. Clark

CHAPTER 15

Even though Mavis' heart and head were heavy with bits and pieces of her dream, she managed to function normally for the next couple of hours.

By seven they were eating a huge breakfast, after which Mavis drove Kim home, then returned to her own house to get ready for Colin. Her biggest concern was being tempted if he smelled like meat, and she was sure he would. After much thought and deliberation, she decided to take a small jar of menthol rub with her; she would smear it under her nose to block his scent. If he asked, she would simply tell him she was a bit congested. After all, she had seen several television programs where cops and morticians and others used menthol rub to deal with the smell of a dead body, so certainly it would work on the smell of a live one.

She wore regular jeans and a black sweatshirt with Heavy Metal written on the front in white letters, with a trademark skull. After donning her combat boots and black leather jacket, she then tucked a single slab of liver in a baggie and tucked it into the inside pocket of her jacket. Grabbing her purse and cell, Mavis looked at the time: a quarter of nine. Time to go out with her mother and wait.

"Do you have any plans for this afternoon?" Jane asked when she entered the kitchen. "We aren't going to Grandma's until four, so you'll have a few hours to burn once you get home."

"Yeah," Mavis said lightly. "I think I'll drive into Toledo and go to the mall; I want to use the gift certificate Kim got me."

"Good plan," her mother agreed. "Now, we won't be home when you get back, so make sure when you leave again you lock the house. You drive safely, Mavis. It wouldn't do to have to make an insurance claim so soon on that car or to pick out a casket for you, for that matter. No texting and driving! Phone on silent when behind the wheel, got that?"

"Yes, ma'am."

Jane looked at her daughter, then bent down and planted a kiss on her cheek. "I love you; have fun today. I have to go shower. See you later."

When she was gone, Mavis called Kim and told her she was going shopping, then reminded her that she promised to come along. Kim agreed, and they decided that Mavis would pick her up at twelve. They would go to a fast food place for lunch, and they would use the drive-thru, now that they could.

No sooner did she hang up, then the doorbell rang: Colin Handley. Mavis' stomach gave a nervous leap. Wow, she hoped she didn't eat him. She quickly smeared menthol rub under her nose and went to the door. Forcing a smile, she grabbed the knob and opened the door.

"Good morning!" she exclaimed cheerfully.

Colin's eyes immediately lit up. "Good morning yourself! I take it you're ready?"

"Yep!" Mavis stepped outside and closed the door behind her. "Did you see what I got for my birthday?" She pointed at the shiny car in the driveway.

"No kidding?" The pair walked to the car, and Colin took a minute to check it out. "Very cool; brand new, too!" He gestured toward the old pickup parked behind her little sedan. "I had to save up for mine. I have too many brothers and sisters, my parents couldn't afford it. I love it, though!"

They climbed into the truck and buckled in while Colin started the engine; suddenly he paused. "Do you smell menthol rub?"

Mavis laughed nervously. "Oh, it's me. I've been a little congested, so I smeared a little under my nose. Hope it doesn't bother you."

Colin laughed and put the truck in reverse. "Not at all. As a matter of fact, it's kind of nice. Reminds me of when I was a kid."

Mavis laughed back. Talk about dodging a bullet! She was getting better and better at thinking ahead.

They tooled down the road, Colin talking about the animal shelter. "They'll be nice and clean, and we only really play with the ones that they know are good-natured. You're not afraid of dogs, are you?"

Mavis shook her head. "No! I love them! My dad's allergic to their dander, which is the only reason we don't have one. It's a bummer, because my mom loves them, too."

The conversation then turned to all the boys at school who had been asking her out. "Are they still bothering you?" Colin asked.

"No, not really," she replied.

"Good," he said with a smile as he pulled into the Humane Society parking lot. "The less competition, the better."

Soon they were parked and headed inside. Mavis was a bit nervous, but she took comfort in the fact that she hadn't gotten a single whiff of Colin since he arrived at her door. Maybe the menthol rub was the true solution; maybe she could begin to put her shame and worry behind her when it came to her weird craving.

They walked inside the small brick building. Dogs were barking like mad everywhere, and the sound made Mavis smile. Sure, the place smelled like a wet pooch, but the barking that echoed through the place made up for the smell.

A plump, pleasant-looking woman in her mid-thirties was sitting behind a glass partition tapping away at a computer. When the pair approached her station, she looked up, a smile spreading across her face. Mavis saw Colin smile back.

"Good morning, Peggy," Colin greeted. "Learn any new tricks, you old dog you?"

The woman chuckled. "Not any that I feel comfortable telling you about." She glanced at her watch. "On time, as usual, I see. I would love it if just once you were late; that way I could play solitaire for a few more minutes each morning."

"Peggy, this is Mavis, the girl I was telling you about." Colin gestured in her direction.

Peggy grabbed a clipboard and looked at Mavis. "Well, hello, young lady! I sure have heard a lot about you! So, are you ready to play with some dogs?"

Mavis nodded shyly. "Sure."

The woman went through a door in her workstation and came around to where they stood. She flipped through the papers on her clipboard, then smiled again. "Okay, today it looks like it's time for Max, Trooper, Digger, and Ace to play in the courtyard." She looked up and made eye contact with Mavis. "They get to play one at a time, for twenty minutes apiece. All four of them are sweethearts; you won't have to worry about them at all."

They began walking down a long hallway, and the barking got louder. About halfway down, the walls turned into ceiling-to-floor caged kennels, each holding either one or two dogs. Some barked, others panted with the excitement of seeing people.

At the second cage on the left, a small terrier of some kind sat in the corner. He wasn't barking or panting, and he kept his distance from the cage door, unlike the others. Mavis stopped and looked at him; he had terribly sad eyes and seemed to cower at the slightest attention.

Peggy and Colin had continued walking and talking, but soon Colin noticed that Mavis had paused. He backed up and stood next to her, with Peggy right behind him. They both looked in at the heartbroken little guy.

"He's been like this since they picked him up," Peggy said in a low voice. "He doesn't bite, at least, not so far. But he just won't let anyone touch or pet him at all. He's scheduled for termination tomorrow."

"Termination?" Mavis asked, her voice trembling.

"Mmm," Peggy replied. "He's been here a month, and no one has claimed him or shown interest in adoption. Unfortunately, we don't have the funds or the space to keep them forever."

Mavis knelt down and poked her fingers through the chain-link caging. "Oh, little guy. I'm so sorry." Her voice was soothing and sad. The little dog's ears perked up, and she could see his nose twitching. "Come on," she urged. "Come see Mavis."

The white and black little guy timidly took a step, then stopped, sniffing like crazy. "I won't hurt you. Come see me; it's okay, fella." He crept another half-foot, listening to the sound of her voice and sniffing, then three more inches. Soon, he was just out of the reach of her fingers. Mavis knelt even lower, still talking, and poked her nose through the fencing. All at once, the dog came up and put his nose to hers, then started licking her face, his little tail thumping on the floor.

Mavis laughed. "He likes me," she said. Mavis looked up at Colin. "I'm going to take him home; how much to adopt?"

"But your dad…" Colin said in a confused voice.

Mavis shook her head. "It's okay; I'll keep him at my grandmother's. Besides, she loves dogs, and she needs a friend. He'll have a huge yard, and he'll be happy. How much?"

Peggy knit her brow. "Eighty dollars, but that's with a chip and shots. The problem is, you have to be eighteen or have a parent or guardian."

"Then I'll come in the morning, with my mother," she said firmly. "Will you hold him until then? Please?"

Peggy thought about it. "I can put things off one more day, sure."

Mavis beamed and stood up. "I'll be back for you, little fella!"

The dog gave a yap and pressed his face against the gate. As she walked off with Colin and Peggy, the dog began to bark. "I'll be back; I promise."

As the trio continued up the hall, the dogs went nuts. They were barking like mad, some of them even howling like wolves. "What has gotten into you kids today?" Peggy asked cheerfully.

They got to the end of the hall and stopped at the last cage on the right. The paper placard on the cage read 'Max'; beneath that was the name 'Ace.' Inside were a golden retriever and wire-haired terrier; they were surrounded by rubber bones and dog food, with a single pile of poop in the corner.

"Forgive the poo," Peggy said. "The volunteer who cleans the kennels doesn't come in until after lunch. They did have baths last night, so they shouldn't be stinky, though. Ace is the retriever; take him out first."

Colin grabbed a leash from a hook next to the kennel door and pulled the bolt. He entered the cage and began petting both dogs and loving them up. Mavis got a chill just watching; she couldn't wait to spend some time playing with the animals. Colin leashed up the larger dog, reassured the other that he would return for him, and then closed the door and bolted it.

"Follow me, madame," he said to Mavis with a smile.

Right next to the kennel, at the very end of the hall, was a large metal door. Mavis had subconsciously taken it for an emergency exit, but as Colin pushed it open she took notice of the sign hanging on it: Courtyard, it read.

The crisp November air hit her in the face and immediately energized her. For the first ten minutes, they threw a ball around for Ace the retriever, laughing and joking at the good-natured animal's antics and personality. After that, Colin gave Mavis time to pet and love the dog. It was then that Ace began to root around insistently at Mavis' leather jacket, almost as if he were trying to wear it with her.

The liver!

Nervously, Mavis rose. "You know, I think he smells my breakfast. I mean, I didn't wash my hands. Where is the bathroom?"

Colin chuckled. "Right across from Peggy's station, right by the front entrance."

She found the washroom easily enough, and to her delight, it was a single toilet area; no stalls. She locked herself in, removed the baggie of liver, and stared at it for a moment. She couldn't, wouldn't just throw it away. No, she was going to have to eat it right then and there.

So Mavis tore in. She bit and chewed over and over, savoring the bloody flavor. It didn't take her long, and soon she was burying the baggie at the bottom of the trash. When she went to wash her hands at the sink, she caught a glimpse of her reflection: her mouth and chin were all bloody.

"Oh, gosh!" She began to wash her face, then dried it and touched it up with powder. Next, she scrubbed her hands really well and headed back to the courtyard. On her way, as she passed Peggy, she got a strong whiff of raw bacon. She glanced at the woman, who looked up and smiled.

"Having fun?"

Mavis nodded, smiled back, and took off down the hall. She had washed all the menthol rub off. Slowing her pace, Mavis pulled the little container out of her purse, smeared some under her nose, and put it back. She was just reaching the courtyard door when Colin came back in.

"Hey!" he said. "Max's turn!"

So, for the next couple of hours, Mavis and Colin played with the animals, and she had more fun that she had in a long time. When it was time to leave, she stopped to tell her little doggie goodbye, and she reassured him she would be there in the morning to get him. As she was walking away, Colin stopped her.

"So, you're going to skip school in the morning for that little guy, huh?" he asked.

Mavis nodded. "Absolutely."

The pair left the shelter in high spirits, and soon they were pulling up in her drive. Colin put the truck in park and turned the radio down. Oh, no, Mavis thought. Here it comes.

"So," he began. "I'm not going to be overbearing by trying to kiss you or anything." Mavis sighed with relief. "I just wanted you to know I had fun. Hopefully, we can go out again?"

Mavis nodded shyly. "Sure. I'm just a 'take things slow' kind of person."

"Me too."

He walked her to her door, then asked her if she wanted to go out for pizza sometime. Mavis eagerly agreed, and they said their goodbyes. She stood, watching him walk to his truck. She couldn't just let him go without some kind of reassurance, could she?

"Colin!"

He turned around eagerly as if hoping she would stop him. Mavis smiled at him, and he smiled back. He was so good-looking.

"Yeah?" he asked.

Mavis shrugged. "Call me, okay?"

"Wild horses couldn't keep me from it, Mav."

With that, Colin Handley jumped into his truck, gave two brief honks and a wave, and drove away.

∞

"So, Mom," Mavis said into her cell as she gnawed on a cold pork chop, "I'm getting ready to go shopping with Kim. Do you need anything?"

"No dear, but thanks for letting me know," Jane replied. "Did the date go well?"

"The 'appointment' was fine," Mavis confirmed. "By the way, I'm adopting a dog tomorrow morning, so I'll be late for school. Oh, and I need you to come with me because I'm not eighteen."

Jane took in a deep breath. "Mavis, your father!"

"I know," she said reassuringly. "I'll keep him at Grandma's, and I'll go every day to care for him, I promise. Mom, they were going to kill him; I couldn't leave him there."

"But…"

"I'll pay for the food, and I'll be super-responsible," she said. "Please!"

Jane groaned. "We'll talk about it later; that's all I can say for now."

Mavis smiled; that was basically a yes. "Yay! Thank you! See you later." She hung up before her mother could change her mind, then ran out of the house. After making sure the place was secured, she hit the road and went to Kim's; time to go shopping.

"Whoa," Kim stated as she climbed in and fastened her seatbelt. "I can't believe we have a car! How cool is this?"

"I know, right?" Mavis put the little vehicle into gear. "Let's hit it!"

The afternoon was good. First, the girls stopped and had fried chicken and biscuits from 'Legz n Thingz' restaurant, eating in instead of going through the drive-thru as they had planned. They wanted to spend time gabbing about Colin Handley and Shawn, Kim's boyfriend, so eating inside was a much better option.

After that, they hit the mall, where Mavis proceeded to spend her entire gift certificate on all things black. The place was a bit pricey, so she got only four outfits, but she loved each and every one of them. She even got Kim a pair of little earrings that were the letter 'K.'

The afternoon went all too quickly, and soon Mavis' watch read two thirty. They headed for Kim's house with high spirits and good moods. When they pulled up out front, Kim turned to her.

"I'm glad you had a good birthday," she said, patting her friend on the arm. "Whatever has been bothering you, it will clear up."

"Why do you think something is bothering me?" Mavis asked.

Kim shrugged and got out, then leaned down to finish the conversation. "I've known you my whole life; I just know, that's all. So, I'll expect you to pick me up on time in the morning, Jeeves."

"Yes, madame!"

As Mavis drove home, she thought about what Kim had said. Could her friend really tell that something was bothering her? Yes, she probably could, but Mavis wasn't ready to confide. Actually, she thought she never would be.

She didn't want to think about it, and quickly put it out of her mind. Now, time to go home and wait for her parents. The day was only half over; they still had Grandma Cabot and Sunday dinner to contend with.

CHAPTER 16

"Mavis, I just don't know," Jane mused as she sat in her rocker with her coffee. "I mean, your father does have pills for his dog allergy, but you know how he hates to take pills! The only time he has to take them now is if we visit friends or relatives with dogs, or if someone with a dog is too close to him. And he complains like a tired toddler with every pill he takes; I hate it!"

Mavis sat on the couch, peeling the label off a bottle of water. "I know, Mom, but if you could just see this little guy, and they're going to murder him! Slaughter him! Just like cattle, or some kind of sacrifice! It's horrible!"

Jane sipped her coffee and chuckled. "It's not quite like that, Mavis."

"Mom, I'll just call Grandma and ask her to go."

Jane set her coffee cup down and turned fully to her daughter. "Mavis, even if it lived at Grandma's your father would have to take pills every day. You said you would go and play with it and feed it daily. Well, you'll be bringing its hair and dander home on your clothes, and... well... I just don't know."

Mavis thought it was strategic to be silent right then. She wadded up the paper label and, after draining the remainder of the water, shoved the little paper ball down inside the bottle and recapped it. She may have looked nonchalant, which was her intent, but she had her mother in her peripheral vision and her ears peeled.

After a few minutes, Jane sat forward again. "I'll tell you what, and this is really your only option: I'll talk to your dad... sometime between now and before he leaves for work. He'll either agree to take his pills and live with a dog, or he won't. And that's really that, Mavis."

Jane had a look of both compassion and remorse on her face, and Mavis believed her. "I think I'm going to write Daddy a note of my own and put it at his place at the kitchen table; would that help any?"

Her mother shrugged. "It couldn't hurt."

Mavis stood up and gave her mother a kiss. "I'll go do that, and then I'm hitting the sack. I love you, and thanks, Mom."

"I love you, too."

For the next hour, Mavis locked herself in her room and penned a short letter to her father, then ate some liver to calm her belly. When she went out to put the letter at her father's chair, she could hear her parents talking in their room. Mavis left the letter, but she already knew the dog was as good as hers.

Before going to bed for the night, she quickly checked to see if her parents were still awake. After standing silently outside their bedroom door and verifying their individual snores, Mavis went back to the kitchen. A quick check of the fridge told her there was a gallon baggie with thawed hamburger patties in it, almost a dozen. Mavis carefully snuck one out and practically inhaled it in one bite; it was delicious!

Finally, with a smile on her face, she snuggled under her blankets and drifted off to sleep.

∞

Just as Mavis suspected, her father gave in to her desires and allowed her to have the dog.

On Monday morning, her mother called her in late to school, and the two of them headed down to the humane shelter. There, they filled out all the adoption paperwork and paid the required fees. They put the terrified little dog into her mother's back seat, hoping that he wouldn't have an accident, and made their way to All Pets pet store. They purchased a kennel, several toys, including a ball and a squeaky, fuzzy lamb. They also bought food and water bowls and potty pads to use until he was housebroken.

On the way home, Mavis held the little guy on her lap. For the entire drive, he tugged on the drawstring at the bottom of her winter coat, growling and pulling on it as if it were a cat's tail, and the cat was trying to get away. It was hugely entertaining, and both Jane and Mavis found themselves laughing long and hard at his antics.

"He sure is feisty," Mavis said.

Jane studied the dog for a brief moment at a stop light. "I think that's a perfect name for him: Feisty.

What do you think?"

Mavis held him up and studied his little face, his tongue darting out and tagging her nose.

"Feisty it is," she confirmed with a giggle. "Welcome home, Feisty!"

They drove two more blocks, and Jane said, "By the way, Mav. I seriously think you should consider studying law in college."

Mavis turned to her, confused. "Why?"

"Well," Jane replied, "that letter you wrote your father about getting this dog convinced him so well that he had tears in his eyes. I'm pretty sure you'd defend criminals very well."

Mavis smiled to herself and turned her attention back to Feisty. She knew the letter had been one that would tug on his heartstrings. As a matter of fact, Mavis had intended fully for it to have that effect. Maybe becoming an attorney was a good idea.

But first, she'd have to be sure she wasn't going to eat any of her clients.

CHAPTER 17

For the next few weeks, almost everything in Mavis' life went well. School was a breeze, even though the boys had started asking for dates again. She was able to handle it gracefully after Colin told her to let them know she was spoken for. Even though their relationship was still very platonic, Mavis was more than happy to take him up on the suggestion. Before long, the 'regulars' pretty much gave up, and by the beginning of December, all she had to deal with were mostly freshman stragglers.

As for Colin, yes, they were 'just friends,' but he was very clear that his feelings for her consisted of a bit more than just hanging out and playing Tiddlywinks. He wanted to be 'exclusive.' Mavis was interested in that, too, but for the time being, she knew to keep some sort of distance was best. To Colin, and everyone else, she presented this desire as nothing more than lingering aftereffects of Jeff Deason's untimely demise, and only she knew the truth. It was in Colin's best interest that things remain as they were, at least for the time being. So, the pair began to see each other more often, but Mavis kept a strict rule: no going out alone; they had to be around other people. Their dates consisted of hanging with either his friends, in a public place, or with Kim and Shawn. Colin didn't argue about it at all.

During the last few days in November, Mavis encountered another dilemma: her liver and other raw snacks were simply not doing the trick anymore.

Sure, she found she was satisfied, but only for about twenty minutes to a half-hour at a time. Mavis began to get edgy, and her sense of smell seemed more powerful than ever before in her life. Everyone smelled wonderful and inviting, and she was beginning to think she was going to have to spend the rest of her life smearing crap under her nose. As a matter of fact, she considered actually taking out stock in the menthol rub company when she turned eighteen.

Mavis lost a lot of sleep over the issue. She was at the end of her rope; she was concerned for everyone she cared about and even found herself concerned for most of the complete strangers she encountered, once she got a whiff of their seeming deliciousness. She came very close, on more than one occasion, to going to her mother and spilling her guts. It was lucky for her that, on the very day she finally made a firm decision to do just that, she came across the solution she had been looking for.

It was a cold Saturday. Mavis' symptoms had become so overwhelming that she had begun to subtly isolate herself from everyone, even Kim. On that particular morning, the sun was shining brightly, and the crisp air was both therapeutic and refreshing. She decided to get into her car, drive around aimlessly, and think.

She wound up on a gravel road just outside of Greenville. There were patches of woods and several pieces of farmland and farmhouses scattered here and there, and she discovered that, due to the low temperatures, she was pretty much the only person on the road. They'd had one big snowfall two days before, but even the gravels were stable enough to drive on, but the only other vehicles she saw were pickup trucks.

At one point, Mavis pulled over to the side of the road to answer a text from her mother. When she had finished, she looked up to see that she had parked near a large patch of woods. Mavis went to put her car into gear to pull away when an old pickup truck pulled up and parked on the opposite side of the road. Her phone rang. It was her mother, so she answered, her eyes glued to the man inside the truck.

As she listened to her mother tell her about her parents' plans to go out that night, and how dinner was in the fridge to be warmed up, Mavis saw the man get out of his truck. Her mother was rattling on, but Mavis didn't hear a word she said. She was paying attention to the guy as he fished around in the back of the truck.

He stood his back to her, seemingly oblivious to his surroundings. Jane rambled on, but Mavis' eyes were glued to the stranger. Next, he lifted out some items made of metal, then turned, nodded in Mavis' direction and smiled, then headed across the road and through the small field to the woods. All at once, Mavis realized what the man had pulled out of the back of his truck.

Traps!

"Yeah, that's nice, Mom," Mavis mumbled.

Jane growled. "Are you even listening to me? I told you that you don't need to feed Feisty anything tonight. He's eating too much, too late in the day. Your father says that's why he's pooping during the night."

"Sure, I heard you," Mavis replied, snapping back to attention. "No extra food for Feisty."

Feisty had turned out to be a huge blessing for the Harvey family. He was full of spit and vinegar and personality, and it didn't take long after bringing him home that the entire family fell totally in love with him, even Todd. In no time at all, the man was eagerly taking his allergy medication to ease the sting of Feisty's presence, and he even took him out to play Frisbee a few times a week. Next, to Mavis, Todd was high up on Feisty's 'best pal' list, and it was increasingly obvious with each passing day that Todd regarded Feisty in much the same way.

There was only one problem with Feisty: the way he smelled to Mavis. If she played with him for too long, he began to smell like a little roasted piglet, and that freaked her out. She loved him, and the last thing she wanted to do was turn him into a meal during some blind hunger rampage. So, true to her word, she fed him, walked him, and played with him faithfully, but she did so with big gobs of menthol rub shoved up each nostril.

Ugh.

"Good," Jane concluded. "So anyway, we won't be home until very late, so don't wait up. We're going to be heading to Cleveland to catch that holiday symphony, and if I know the Masons, Rob and Kathleen will want to stop for some kind of ice cream or dessert before heading back to Toledo. We likely won't be home until one-thirty, two o'clock in the morning."

"Fine. Listen, Mom, I have to go," Mavis said. "I'll see you tomorrow."

They disconnected, and Mavis looked back toward the woods for the man with the traps, but he was gone. She really didn't care about that, but she would have liked to have watched him set one or two of them. She was very curious, all of a sudden, about how they worked.

The truth was, a trap or two just might be the solution to her growing appetite problem. Perhaps, just perhaps, if she were to set a couple of traps, she would be able to have some actual warm, nearly-alive meat for herself. Maybe, just maybe, it would appease the monster that seemed to be living and growing ever-stronger inside of her.

Mavis threw the little sedan into gear, whipped a U-turn in the middle of the gravel road, and started back for Greenville. Now she was smiling, and the trap idea gave her new hope.

Time to head for Otis' Outdoorsman Shop.

∞

"So, little miss, what are you interested in trapping?" Mavis stood at the Trap Goods counter at Otis'

Outdoorsman, staring at the two different traps that the salesman had set before her. They were very different, and she had plenty of questions, but for the time being, it seemed the man had a few of his own. After all, Mavis knew she didn't look like your typical tomboy trapper girl.

She knit her brow. "Um, I'm not really sure. You see, I was reading about it, and it really got me interested, you know? I mean, I love the outdoors, and I could certainly use a little extra money, and the pelt would give me that." She paused and continued to study the traps. Finally, Mavis smiled and shrugged. "I guess I need a lot of help."

For the next hour, the man, who reminded her a bit of her father, talked to her about the basic ins and outs of trapping. He discussed different animals, the best traps, and they discussed the use of foods as a lure. By the time they were finished, Mavis had a boatload of education, two new traps, and a few extras. He even gave her advice on where to set them, but she already had a great location in mind: her backyard.

The Harveys' backyard was very large, and it had a high privacy fence all around it. The family didn't spend very much time back there, but Jane usually kept it very nice, with furnishings and a classy fire pit, in case they decided to entertain outdoors during the warmer seasons. But the best part about the yard was all the greenery. There was a small maze of trees, a bunch of lilac bushes, and a variety of other lush plant life, including many species that stayed green and full, even during the winter.

In the farthest corner from the house, the plants and trees were the thickest. They were so thick, in fact, that no one ever really ventured in. A variety of animals could be seen all year round, including squirrels and rabbits. The rabbits mostly came through a small gap between the fence and the house, toward the front, but once they were in, they stayed.

It was in that thick greenery that Mavis intended to set her traps.

When she got home, her parents were already gone, so Mavis got to work. Within forty-five minutes she had the job done; the traps were set and waiting. Now, all she could do was wait.

She showered and ate, then got her cell out of her room. Mavis saw that she had missed two calls from Kim and one from Colin. She quickly slimed down a slab of liver, noted that she needed more (hoping that she wouldn't need much more if the trap idea worked), and sat down in her dad's recliner to return the calls. First, she would call Kim; her friend didn't even say hello when she answered.

"Oh, my goodness! I tried to call you twice, and even went to the house!" Her friend sounded frustrated. "Your car was there, but you didn't answer the bell; where are you?"

"Sorry. Jeesh, I must have been in the shower," Mavis lied. "What's wrong?"

Kim groaned. "We were supposed to hook up this morning to go online for dresses for the Winter

Formal!"

Mavis sat back and put her feet up. "Oh, yeah... I forgot. Besides, I said Colin asked me, but I didn't accept yet." She didn't mention that she intended to do just that as soon as she hung up from her friend's call.

Kim wasn't hearing it. "Don't move! I'm coming over!"

The girl didn't even say goodbye, which made Mavis chuckle. Kim was on to her, and she was likely a bit perturbed that Mavis hadn't been keeping her up to date on personal information regarding her love life. Clearing her mind and her smile, Mavis shook her head and dialed Colin. She took a deep breath; hopefully, he wasn't as irked as Kim.

"Hey, Mavis!"

He sounded cheerful. "Sorry I missed your call," she said. "I had my hands full. What's up?"

Colin paused. "Well, I'm not trying to be pushy. You know I wouldn't do that. But... my dad's taking me to Mr. Spiffy tomorrow to rent a... you know. A tux. For the dance. But you hadn't..." His voice trailed off.

What the heck, Mavis thought. Sure, she was nervous, but they certainly wouldn't be alone at the dance. She would make sure they stayed in the mix, and if all else failed, it would be menthol rub to the rescue. At this point, it would be wrong to let him down; the dance was in just over two weeks.

"Sure, Colin," she replied with a smile. "I'll go with you to the Winter Formal."

"You will?" He was excited.

Mavis laughed. "Yeah. Go ahead and get your tux."

He laughed with relief. "Awesome! Okay, I'm at Saturday practice, so I'd better go. Call you later?"

"You'd better."

The pair quickly said their goodbyes, and Mavis reached for the remote control. As she surfed the television channels, she thought about the fact that she had accepted Colin's request that she go to the dance with him. Regardless of her concerns, she was happy and felt like she did the right thing.

Mavis found a rerun of her favorite show, *The Cravens*, and settled in. No sooner did she get comfortable than Kim flew through the front door. Mavis barely moved, only turned her head.

"Hey," she greeted her friend.

Kim began to take off her coat. "So, listen. I've been thinking. You're my best friend, you know? Whether you go to the dumb dance or not, I'm going, so you should be willing to help me. I would do it for you!" She hung her coat in the closet and plopped down on the couch. "You're so weird lately. I don't even know what to think. Where's your laptop?"

"In my room," Mavis said casually.

Kim stood up dramatically. "Aargh!" she growled and stomped off down the hall. She returned with the computer, set it on the coffee table, and booted it up. "Man, if you were going, and I weren't, I would at least pretend to be excited for you... Jeesh!"

"I don't have to pretend," Mavis replied. "I'm going to the dance with Colin."

Kim jerked her eyes from the computer screen. "Really?"

Mavis nodded. "Hold on… this is almost over. I want to see the end."

They sat in silence watching the end of *The Cravens*. Mavis laughed at all the dumb jokes, while Kim squirmed impatiently on the sofa. When the credits began to roll, Mavis put the recliner in the upright position, turned the set off, and turned to Kim.

"So, what do you think of something black with, like, glitter snowflakes all over the bottom part of the gown? You know how I feel about black lately. It's not the most Christmassy of colors, but if you add some scattered glitter, voila!"

Kim stared at her. "You're really starting to piss me off."

Mavis laughed silently to herself. She was getting more and more entertained by getting her best friend all worked up. Seeing Kim squirm and hearing her growl was quickly becoming the highlight of each and every day. Her friend was so stressed out lately for some reason; she needed to relax and lighten up.

The girls spent the next two hours looking over dresses online, and finally, they settled on a bare-shouldered number with a fitted bodice and gauzy, fluffy gown with silver glitter, which gave the impression of winter and snow. The dress came in either white, black, or red. Kim opted for red, and of course, Mavis eagerly chose the black. At first, she was worried about her shoulders, but she had a gauzy black shawl with silver sequins that would take care of the problem.

Kim had her mother's credit card, so while she ordered hers, Mavis bookmarked the page on her computer, then jotted down all the information on the dress so her mother could order it. Jane would be ecstatic that she had accepted Colin's invitation, and Mavis knew she would love the dress as well.

When they were finished, Mavis piled a frozen pizza high with crumbled bacon and extra cheese, then popped it into the oven. She had invited Kim to stay overnight since her parents were out, but as it turned out, her friend was going out with Shawn after practice. So, they watched part of a movie, ate the pizza, and then Mavis drove Kim to Westside High to meet Shawn.

With Kim out of the car, Mavis drove home a little faster than she should have; she was eager to check her traps.

R.W.K. Clark

CHAPTER 18

Monday was the beginning of a very busy week for the students of Westside High. Midterms were to begin that week, which had almost everyone on edge, and the dance was a mere two weeks away. Those two things were all anyone talked about, it seemed. Everyone was eager for both, for the simple reason that the day of the dance was also the first day of winter vacation.

Mavis' junior year was almost half over.

While she was excited about it, she had other things on her mind that she was more preoccupied with, one of them being Colin Handley. They were hanging out quite often, but always with other people. Colin, however, didn't seem too distressed by their lack of alone time. Mavis, on the other hand, was beginning to toy with the idea more and more every day. She had only just agreed to go to the dance with him, and already she found herself toying with the idea of maybe… making out, just a little bit. After all, he was so cute. She could only imagine what a real kiss from Colin would feel like.

She was sitting in first-period Literature. Having just completed her midterm, which covered the novels they had read during the semester, Mavis was lost in her thoughts. She had a book open on the desk, to look busy, but her mind was far from Miss Hawkins' dusty classroom.

She shifted her thoughts from Colin to the traps. On both Saturday night and late Sunday night, Mavis checked on them, but she had caught nothing. Early Sunday afternoon she drove to the market with money Jane had given her for her 'school liver' and stocked back up, but she knew the meat wasn't as effective as it had once been. It was all she could do to hope her traps began to catch something, anything! Late Sunday night she went out and put fresh food down and hoped for the best.

Now here it was, Monday. Mavis also had the midterm on her mind as well. She wasn't worried about her grade; Mavis had always been able to pull off top-notch grades with little to no effort; she considered herself blessed, in that way. But the midterm had been almost too easy; there were several questions that she didn't even read half-way through, and she was already beginning to jot down the answers. While her body seemed to be paling and spotting slightly a little more every day, her mind seemed sharp, at least to her. The midterm had pretty much proven it. When she had finished, she read over her work quickly, and Mavis found her answers to not only be correct but highly articulate, as well.

Now she was considering the whole mind and body thing. Mavis had stood naked before the full-length mirror just last week. It had been the first time in weeks that she had done so, having purposely been avoiding it. Ever since the gray spots sort of flaked off of her body in chunks, Mavis tried to avert her eyes as much as possible. If anything bothered her about this supposed anemia, it was that symptom. Deep inside, though, Mavis knew that she no more suffered from anemia than she was able to fly. Something much more intense, and a bit scarier was going on. She just didn't want to deal with it.

So, last week she bucked up and stood in front of the mirror. She was covered in the spots; they were sprinkled here and there, scattered over her skin as if someone had flung drops of acid on her. Mavis had touched several of them. All of them were rough to the touch; some only a light, surface roughness, others hard in the center, as if the spot was rooted deep in her skin. Mavis didn't pick at any of them; she just gently applied some moisturizing lotion and stuffed the slight fear she felt down deep into her being. For some reason, she felt strongly that the spots were not something she could go to her mother about.

Besides, Mavis felt fine!

The bell rang loudly and suddenly, jolting Mavis out of her thought-induced trance; the class had seemed to fly by. She quickly jumped up and gathered her things, then bolted out and made her way to the stairs to meet Kim. As she neared the stairway, she saw that Colin was waiting for her.

"Hey!" she greeted him. She stood on her toes and

planted a kiss on his cheek, then backed away in time to enjoy watching him blush. "I have to meet Kim; I wasn't expecting to run into you."

"I'll walk you." They started off, Colin grinning like crazy. "Listen, I'm really happy that we're going to the dance together. Does this mean I can consider us 'official'?"

Mavis almost choked on her own spit. "Um, not quite." After forcing a pleasant chuckle, she continued. "Let's just see if we make it through the next two weeks and then the dance without either of us, um, killing the other one."

Colin gave a loud guffaw. "You're funny, Mavis."

Mavis gave a small laugh and rolled her eyes; if only he knew how serious she really was!

"Look, there's Kim!" Mavis grabbed Colin by the arm and stopped him, then planted another peck on his cheek. "Call me later if you want, okay?"

Colin's hand went to his cheek, and he blushed again. "Sure thing. Talk to you later."

"You two are getting mighty chummy," Kim teased when Mavis got to her. "Oh, by the way, my mom's picking me up after school. I have to go have my teeth cleaned so you won't have to drive me."

"Okay." Secretly, Mavis was relieved. Now she could get home and change and check her traps without any distractions. Her mother had told her that she would be at one of her volunteer jobs until almost five; Mavis was to check the pot roast that was in the crockpot and turn it down, but otherwise, she would be free and clear. She had a good feeling about the traps for some reason; her gut told her she had caught something. Mavis hoped it wasn't a bony old squirrel, but if it were, she wouldn't look a gift squirrel in the mouth, or whatever the saying was.

She only had one more midterm that day: Social Studies. Once that class, which she attended during third period, was over, all she had to do was get through German and PE… no problem. Mavis had been changing in the bathroom stall since she first noticed the veins and spots, and since it was her last class, she just showered at home in the evening. The rest of the day would be a breeze.

But things didn't go quite as quickly as they had for the first half of that Monday. The German teacher, Mr. Lindsay, decided to have a pre-midterm oral exam, which gave everyone present cause to groan. Mr. Lindsay's idea of an oral exam was a series of small skits, each with different students, and each ad-libbed entirely by them in German. He would call the students for each skit to the front of the room, give them a rough plot, and ten minutes. One would think they would be quite funny, but the fact was, most of the students in Mavis' sixth-period German class seemed to be suffering from massively traumatic stage fright. Every oral exam that year had nearly required the use of a hearing aid for the students who were left to observe. Mavis thought a bullhorn on the part of the examinees was appropriate.

Needless to say, the clock hands seemed frozen for

the entire hour.

It was a struggle, but at three fifteen Mavis actually experienced the jubilation of hearing the last bell go off. She practically ran to her locker, and she definitely speed-walked to her car. Once she was out of the student lot, she let out a huge breath.

At last, she was free to go home and check the stupid traps that had been distracting her all day.

CHAPTER 19

Mavis' gut had given her correct information; when she got home, one of her traps had been sprung.

But she had also been right when she thought about a scrawny squirrel, which was just what she had gotten. The little fellow was so fresh and frightened he was twitching when she found him. Immediately, Mavis' appetite alarm went off, the scent of the animal driving her mad as soon as she picked it up. As a matter of fact, she wasn't even three steps in the door when she smelled him; she dropped her things and ran out back.

Mavis ended up sitting in the snow, hidden by the clump of greenery which also covered the traps, eating like a crazy person. The hiding didn't bother her, and neither did the fact that she had on one of her new outfits and a favorite winter coat. She spent twenty minutes chowing down, and when she was finished, she threw the carcass over the fence, giving a loud burp but not a second thought.

Mavis headed back inside, stopping just before she reached the back door to look at her hands. They were covered in blood and bits of fur, and a quick look at the rest of her body revealed that her clothes were, too. She gave a groan, then pulled her coat sleeve over her hand and opened the back door, trying to keep from getting blood on the knob as best as she could.

Once she was back inside, Mavis made sure all the doors were locked. She went into the basement and stripped down, then saturated all of her clothes in liquid oxygen-based stain remover, reminding herself to put the item on the shopping list; her mother would kill her for using the last of it without making a note. Next, she stuffed all of the items into the washing machine, including her coat, and as she started the machine, she thanked her lucky stars that she had been wearing all black.

With that task done, Mavis streaked through the house at full speed, running right for the shower. A quick look in the bathroom mirror told her that she had blood in her hair and all over her face. With a groan, Mavis turned on the water, checked the temperature, and jumped in.

As she soaped up and scrubbed, Mavis noted that she was full of energy, almost high, in fact. She was done with her shower in no time. Then she dressed, blow-dried her hair, and went back out to reset her trap. One squirrel, every couple of days, wasn't going to do the trick; either things were going to have to pick up, or she would have to buy more traps. Maybe she should do that anyway, and set them off in the woods somewhere like that guy had out on the gravel road.

When Mavis went back into the house, Jane was home.

"Hey! How was your day?" her mother greeted.

Mavis smiled nervously. "Good. How about yours?"

"Fine… just fine." Jane started to make a pot of coffee. "What were you doing outside?"

As she removed her coat, Mavis glanced back through the sliding glass door. "Oh, nothing. Just watching the birds, that's all."

"Aren't they beautiful?" Jane checked the dishwasher to see if it needed to be run. "Are you hungry?"

Mavis laughed. "Always."

"I'll whip something up."

After a pause, Mavis said, "Thanks. I'm going to go hit the books really quick. Call me when the food's done?"

Her mother gave her a pleasant nod, so she headed for her room. The truth was, Mavis didn't have any homework at all; she just needed a minute alone to process things. She felt like she had drunk a pot of coffee; her skin was tingling, her hair was standing on end, and she had enough energy to run a mile in less than a minute. The last time she had felt like that was after the incident with… Jeff and the mole. She knew that it was because her little squirrelly snack had still been alive when she dug in. The life force seemed to be what got her all amped up, and she knew it.

The liver would never satisfy her again; it was definitely time to step up her trapping game.

So, for the next half-hour, instead of doing homework, like she told Jane, Mavis did some research on trapping. She read up on lures and different animals and areas, and by the time she was finished, she knew she was probably going to have to set her traps in another area. The backyard simply wasn't going to give her the variety she obviously needed.

By the time her mother yelled down the hall to tell her the food was ready, Mavis felt like she might have a chance at meeting her own 'nutritional' needs. Sure, the day-to-day food she had been eating her entire life would fill her up, but she knew that fresh, living food was what she needed to make her feel like she was on top of her game. She was simply going to have to adjust her sails in accordance with the winds of change that were blowing on her.

∞

After supper that evening with her parents, Mavis told them she was going to the strip mall. She geared up, drove herself to Otis' Outdoorsman Shop, and purchased two more traps, along with some very specific lures and some trap tags. Now it was time to head to her chosen spot.

There was a patch of woods near Grandma Cabot's house that Mavis used to play in when she was much younger. Back then, there had been a couple of kids her age who lived on her grandmother's street, and the three of them would go traipsing through those woods for hours on end during the day. She even remembered building a fort out of sticks and leaves with them; the memory made her smile as she drove.

That was where she planned to set up shop. On

second thought, it was too late to take care of business right then, though she would have loved to. Mavis knew she would have to wait for the next day. She planned to go to the woods immediately after school the following day. Waiting would allow her enough time to do what she needed to do. Then she could check the traps after school every day.

As she drove home, Mavis thought about her plans. For the first time in her life, she was going to end up lying to her friend Kim. There was no way that she could go about her business with her best friend in tow, so Mavis planned to tell her that she would be helping her grandmother after school for the next couple of weeks. She felt bad, but there was nothing she could do. This was not a want, as far as Mavis was concerned; it was definitely a need.

When she got home, both Jane and Todd were lying in bed with their television set on. Mavis locked the house up behind her and stopped at their room long enough to tell them she was home. Rather than grab a snack from the kitchen, she ate some of her liver in the safety of her room, which seemed to her like eating plain, cold oatmeal. There was hardly any satisfaction at all in eating it, other than the fact that it put something in her stomach. Afterward, as she lay in bed waiting for sleep to come, Mavis knew that this appetite thing wasn't getting any better at all.

In fact, it was getting much, much worse.

CHAPTER 20

That night, Mavis had another dream.

She was in her room, working on homework and listening to heavy metal music. Her parents were in bed, but Mavis could hear them snoring loudly through the wall, the sound echoing as if they were sleeping in a cave. She ignored it and turned the music up louder.

That was when she heard a faint squeaking noise, much like that of a mouse. Mavis stopped and strained her ears to listen again; there! There it is! What is that?

She grabbed the remote to the television and muted the sound. Squeak, squeak! Yes, she could definitely hear it. But as she listened closely, Mavis knew that the sound was not inside the house at all; it was coming from the backyard.

She had caught something in her traps!

Without putting on so much as slippers, or even a robe, Mavis left her room and crept up the hall quietly. She made her way to the kitchen, then to the sliding glass door, which she gently unlocked. Next, she began to slowly creep across the backyard in the darkness. She could feel the snow on her feet, cold and icy, and here and there a twig would poke the tender flesh of her soles. The squeaking noise grew much louder.

She crossed the pitch-black yard with a slow, but sure, pace. She could clearly see everything around her, just as though the sun were beating down. Mavis walked across the snow-covered grass, stopping briefly just before the greenery. After a quick look back at the dark and silent house, Mavis knelt down to crawl into the hidden space where her traps were. Now she could see that the squeaking thing was struggling as it stood in the trap.

A smile crept over Mavis' face. "Hey, there," she said in a soothing voice. "You look like dinner!"

The thing began to cry instead of squeak, and its struggles turned into full-fledged fighting. Mavis grabbed the trap and pulled it close. She was eager to see what was on the menu. As Mavis turned the trap with the creature around, shock took over her entire being…

A tiny, squirming Kim Coleman was in the trap.

Something was shaking Mavis hard.

Suddenly, she was no longer in the thicket in the backyard. She was in her room, and she was screaming at the top of her lungs. Jane was sitting on the edge of her bed, hands-on Mavis' shoulders, trying to shake her out of her deep sleep and the dream that was causing her daughter's screams.

As soon as Mavis registered her mother's presence, her screams stopped.

"Oh, my!" Jane pulled Mavis into her arms and embraced her. "You had a horrible dream! You scared me to death!"

Mavis was coming back to reality very quickly now. She saw that her father was standing near her bedroom door, his hair tousled and his eyes tired. He gave a yawn and ran his fingers through his hair.

"So, is Mavis going to live?" He yawned again. "I have to work early tomorrow."

Jane swung her head around and glared at him. "Then, by all means, go!"

Todd mumbled some inaudible word of thanks and left the room. Jane gave a growl and shook her head before turning back to her daughter, her eyes filled with concern. Mavis offered her a weak smile.

"You know, all of this stress is just too much for me." Jane stood. "Your dad's right: you'll live. I'm taking a sedative and going back to bed; my heart is still pounding."

"Sorry, Mom."

As Jane left, Mavis snuggled beneath her blanket again. She glanced at the clock: it was just before two in the morning, and she was wide awake. Hopefully, it wouldn't take her too long to get back to sleep. Reaching over to her nightstand, Mavis switched off her lamp and closed her eyes.

But her mind was racing; what a horrible dream! Oh, wow, the very thought that she had a dream about trapping, and intending to eat, her best friend simply made her stomach turn. She wanted to cry; what the heck was wrong with her, anyway? Maybe there was nothing really wrong with her physically. Maybe she had some kind of mental illness.

Schizophrenia!

That had to be it! Didn't schizophrenia tend to come on right around her age? Oh, what if she was a psychopath? What if she wanted to eat people because she was sick and needed to be locked up?

In near-panic, Mavis switched her lamp back on and grabbed her laptop from the floor next to her bed. She booted it up, then grabbed some liver from her closet and locked her bedroom door. After making a mental note that the little cooler needed ice, she sat down on her bed and logged in.

Mavis sat cross-legged on her bed researching mental illness for so long that by the time she paid attention to her surroundings, the sun was just beginning to come up. A check of the time told her that it was five-thirty in the morning. What seemed like the last several seconds to Mavis turned out to be four hours in reality.

She looked briefly back at the computer screen and thought about what she had read. According to the all-knowing World Wide Web and the information it had given her, Mavis deduced that all of the symptoms she was exhibiting had nothing to do with mental illness. Her head was sharp and clear, and from what she could tell, she had quite a firm grasp on reality, not to mention the fact that she felt remorse for the bad things she had done.

But, after running searches on all of her symptoms, she was able to get some idea of what might be ailing her. It had nothing to do with anemia or mental illness, or even an overly-dry skin condition accompanied by an insatiable appetite for fresh blood and meat. According to the Web, there would be one thing happening to Mavis, and she knew there was no way possible that could be the case.

The Net told Mavis she was probably turning into a zombie.

CHAPTER 21

By Friday morning, Mavis had all but forgotten the information she had read online in the early morning hours of last Tuesday. As time passed, the 'zombie theory,' as she had come to think of it, seemed more and more ridiculous. She set about her week just as she had all the other weeks before it, thinking it was the most ridiculous thing she had ever read.

Perhaps she found it so easy to blow off the weird idea because of her traps. On that Tuesday morning, she snuck out back while her parents were still sleeping, and was delighted to find a small rabbit. She gobbled it up and went in to shower after washing her hands and face with snow. Fortunately, her parents were sound asleep, and she was able to get thoroughly cleaned up without drawing any attention.

Throughout the week she got lucky as well. Mavis was able to easily keep herself going by switching things up just a bit: she would leave the house earlier in the morning to check the traps she set in the woods by Grandma Cabot's; all she had to do was tell her mother that she was pulling extra credit in art, and it all went over smoothly. She also figured out that she had to be careful of her clothing, so she stuffed an old rain slicker in the trunk of her car and wore it to protect her clothing during her little morning snacks. A package of sanitary wipes were also strategically placed in the trunk for clean-up purposes.

At night, either after her parents were sound asleep or while they were out gallivanting with friends, Mavis would take care of checking the traps in the back. It didn't take long for her to get her little routine down to a fine art, and by Thursday it was almost second nature. Mavis was getting used to sneaking around and lying, and it was that fact alone that caused her to feel any remorse at all.

But another thing happened by Thursday as well: Kim made a big stink about Mavis not picking her up for school in the morning.

Initially, Kim hadn't said a word, and Mavis honestly hadn't considered the fact at all. On Wednesday, after school, Kim seemed a bit short and distant when Mavis drove her home, but she chalked it up to some kind of petty spat between Kim and Shawn. But on Thursday, when Kim wasn't waiting for her to walk to second-period Science class with her, Mavis knew something was a bit off kilter; she just wasn't sure what. She made a decision to bring it up to her friend after school.

But Kim wasn't waiting on the front steps of Westside High for her friend. As a matter of fact, Mavis couldn't find her at all. It wasn't until she was driving home that she saw Kim walking alone up the sidewalk, just as they had done so many times together before

Mavis got her new car. When she saw her, Mavis pulled over to the curb right away and rolled down the passenger window, bracing herself against a rush of cold air.

"Hey!" she hollered. "Kim! What's going on? What's wrong?"

Kim stopped and turned stiffly to her. "What do you care?"

Her friend's response immediately blew her away. By the time she snapped out of her state of surprise, Kim was walking down the sidewalk once again. Mavis couldn't believe it, and she was very confused by Kim's behavior.

She pulled forward and caught up with the girl, who glanced in her direction but kept walking. "Kim! Will you just get in the car? If I did something wrong, you have to tell me, or I can't fix it!"

After a couple more steps, Kim stopped once again, took a frustrated breath, and made her way to the car. She got in, buckled up, put the window up, and stared straight ahead. Mavis just sat there looking at her. A horn blew behind them, and Kim turned to her angrily.

"Are you going to drive, or piss off all of Greenville?"

Mavis jumped slightly, then put the car into gear and took off. "So, what's the problem, Kim?"

She thought her friend might try to give her the silent treatment, but that turned out not to be the case at all. No sooner had the question left Mavis' mouth than Kim whirled in her seat, flames in her eyes and smoke practically coming out of her ears. Mavis winced at the sight.

"What's wrong? What?" Kim growled and looked forward again. "You don't show up to pick me up for school since Monday, leaving me to walk in the cold. You don't return any phone calls I make to you, and you don't give me any explanation. You just drive me home from school without having hardly any conversation, then you drop me off so fast it's like you can't wait to get rid of me!"

Mavis was immediately aware of her bad behavior, and she was equally shocked by it. She certainly had blown her friend off all week, and she had also treated her like a burden. Suddenly, she was riddled with guilt; no wonder the girl was furious! Even though Mavis hadn't been aware of it, she had been treating her friend like garbage.

"You're right," she replied, simply and easily, as she parked at a stop sign.

Kim turned to her, surprised. "I am?"

"Yeah. I've been out of line, and I'm sorry."

Kim paused. "But why?"

A sad look came over Mavis' face. She wanted to tell her friend everything, the whole truth, but she knew that the consequences of such a move could be devastating for everyone. She had to keep things as innocent and innocuous as possible.

With a shrug, she answered. "I've been doing a little extra-credit work. I haven't been sleeping well, which has caused a lot of tension at home. My parents are stressed, and I guess I have been doing a lot of thinking about it all. But I swear to you, Kim, none of it has anything to do with you. I love you! You're like my sister!"

"You mean it?" Kim looked as if she was about to break out in tears.

Mavis immediately pulled over to the curb and put the small vehicle in park. She put her arms around her friend and hugged her tightly. "I swear! I really, truly swear! I'll even pinky swear if you want!"

Both girls broke out in loud laughter. "You're so stupid," Kim said as they pulled away from each other. The girl fished a tissue out of her purse and blew her nose loudly. "You know, I expect you to make it up to me. You've caused a lot of heartaches."

"Uh-oh," Mavis muttered as she sat back in her seat. "What does that mean, exactly?"

Kim dabbed at her eyes again and smiled. "I have a date with Shawn tomorrow night, as usual. But I have a problem with my mom."

Mavis wanted to close her eyes, but she was concerned that it would appear to be very uncaring to her already-sensitive friend. "What's wrong with your mom?"

Kim continued as she stuffed her used tissue back into her purse, "she thinks that Shawn and I have been spending too much 'alone' time together. She thinks I'm going to have sex and wind up a pregnant high school drop-out or something. So... we have to either go out together with friends or not at all. You know, a double date."

"Oh, you've got to be kidding me!"

Kim sat forward, a look of borderline panic coming over her face. "Look, I wouldn't ask, but you kind of owe me now. And Mavis, I'll die… just die, if I don't get to see Shawn. During football he's so busy; we have to take what we can get. You have to come!"

Mavis groaned. "So I can be a third wheel?"

Kim shook her head. "No, of course not, silly. You bring Colin and we double-date."

"Ugh." Mavis couldn't believe Kim was roping her in like that. She fished her cell out of her purse. "Whatever, Kim. This is wrong… just so wrong."

"Are you calling him now?"

With a nod, Mavis pulled up Colin's number in her contacts and pushed the call button. His phone rang three times, prompting Mavis to get ready to hang up, relieved. All of a sudden, he answered, and she wanted to slap him for it.

"Hey, Mavis! What a surprise!"

She sank back into her seat. "Hey, Colin." After quickly sticking her tongue out at Kim, she continued. "So, listen, are you busy tomorrow night?"

"What time?" he asked.

She looked at her friend. "What time?"

"Seven!" Kim replied with a brilliant smile.

Mavis rolled her eyes. "Seven-ish?"

"Sure thing!" Colin sounded so excited that Mavis thought he may have crapped his pants. "What do you want to do?"

"Well..." Mavis knew that if she answered the question in full right then, she ran the risk of being parked on the street with the phone to her ear for the next ten or fifteen minutes. "I'm not really sure, but my mother is beeping in; can I call you back in, say, ten minutes? We can put everything together then."

"I'll be eagerly waiting," Colin replied. "I can't wait."

She hung up and put the car in gear, then carefully took off. "So, what are we going to be doing, Kim? Who's driving? You haven't told me anything yet!"

"No problem!" the girl exclaimed. "You guys just hook up and meet us at Sports Burger by 7:30. We'll figure everything out from there."

"Fine." Mavis had resigned herself to the fact. "Now, listen: I'm not ready to be alone with any boys, Kim. You need to stick close by my side all night, or you're going to end up being the one in debt here. Got it?"

Kim giggled. "Got it! Oh, thank you, Mav; thank you, Mom will be relieved."

Mavis pulled up in front of her house. "So, I can't pick you up in the mornings for a while, but going home is still a go, all right?"

Kim, who already had the car door open, suddenly stopped. "How long is a while?"

Mavis gave her a small smile. "Not long; just until I manage to finish off a couple of spare credits, I'm aiming for."

Kim nodded. "I'll see if Mom will drive me; I'll be fine. See you tomorrow, okay?"

"Sounds good."

Mavis backed out of the drive and aimed the car for home. She hated lying, but when it came to telling Kim it wouldn't be long until things were back to normal, she felt like she didn't have a choice. For the time being, things were the way they were. But she knew that soon she was going to have to tweak her routine a bit, or she was going to wind up losing a lifelong friend.

She knew, all too well, that Kim would never understand the truth.

∞

When Mavis got home, the first thing she did was get changed. Next, she called Colin back, explained everything to him in detail regarding their Friday 'double date', and made arrangements to meet up. They decided that Colin would drive to her house, leave his truck, and together they would drive to Sports Burger in Mavis' little car. She told him he could even drive her car if he wanted to.

So, the rest of that Thursday went routinely well for Mavis. In fact, she even felt a little more stable and secure, due to spending hours the night before researching the ever fictional and popular 'zombie.'

Mavis looked at it like this: the chances that she was slowly becoming one of the undead were non-existent. But... what if? Everything she had read during the wee hours of the night between Monday and Tuesday had pointed her toward just that. Even though she was sure that it was all bologna, what would it hurt to spend a little time on the topic finding out all she could? If she would invest the effort, Mavis was positive that she would quickly disprove the stupid theory that had been weighing on her mind ever since the Net suggested it.

Anyway, as far as her current research and her mission to disprove, by eleven-thirty on Thursday night Mavis became convinced wholly of one thing: she was probably, no matter how unreasonable and psychotic it sounded, a zombie.

While several things made her think this, there were also some that could mean she was not. Or at least, not yet. The passage of time would solidify it as being true for sure.

One thing disturbed her and kept her from learning exactly what she was looking for: in all, she found to read and study, no one who was a zombie was at all functional, or aware of what they were doing. This was the single common point that gave her hope to cling to. It gave her enough faith to keep going while she continued to try to figure it all out.

She did manage to find a couple of things that suggested that, if zombies ever really did exist, they might be aware enough to eat animals to survive. If they were ever lost and no one was around to eat, they would probably stuff themselves on whatever they found. Even though such a thought wasn't found in zombie books or movies, it was a relief.

After all of that, however, when she got up for school on Friday morning, the entire zombie idea was out of her mind. It was as if it had never been suggested. Mavis went back to her routine as soon as she woke, and never gave another thought to be a zombie.

In fact, all of her concern over the changes in her life seemed to fade as well. Overnight, Mavis went from stressing over her situation to nearly forgetting about it completely. The funny thing was, she was none the wiser.

Mavis checked her traps, attended classes, and met up with Kim after school. She went home and ate, visited her mom, and got ready for her date. She didn't even pay attention to the spots and veins as if she could no longer see them for herself.

At 6:45 she looked at her watch: time to go out and wait for her last-minute date.

CHAPTER 22

It was fortunate for Mavis that she left her room when she did; Colin wound up ringing the doorbell before she was even all the way into the living room.

She opened the door to see him standing on the porch, beaming. "Hi! I know I'm a little early, but I just couldn't stand to sit around another second at home."

Mavis invited him in, adding that no one was home, and they might as well head out. Colin agreed with her, and Mavis set about locking up the house. As they went down the sidewalk, she noticed that his truck was in the drive behind her car.

"Did you want to take your truck or my car?" she asked.

Colin stopped mid-stride and gave a sheepish grin. "I forgot. Let me park the truck at the curb quick; I'll be right back."

He jogged to his old beast and started her up, and soon he was on his way back to Mavis, who was already sitting in the passenger seat of her little coupe. Colin hopped in, adjusted the seat and mirrors, and buckled up. Mavis watched him, smiling. He sure was a hottie; it was too bad that she had to focus so much on keeping away from boys like him. She could just eat him up, both literally and figuratively.

He turned to her and smiled. Mavis dangled the keys out toward him, and he plucked them from her hand. "The last time I drove a car this new was never."

"Well, there is a first time for everything!" Mavis sat back and fastened her own safety belt.

Colin started the car and pulled out of the driveway. "Sports Burger, right? You know, it's funny, I have never been a fan of their food. Their burgers taste like they are a lot less than meat, you know what I mean?"

Mavis laughed. "Yeah. I can stomach the Soccer Extravaganza and a couple others, but I would have to agree with you."

Ten minutes later they were pulling into the packed parking lot at Greenville's most popular teen hangout, next to Zander Point. A long line of cars were waiting for drive-thru services, and almost all of the parking spots were full, except for a couple in the back. As they slowly made their way around the maze of kids milling around, Mavis pointed at a rusty, older car.

"There is Shawn's car; they're already inside." Mavis chuckled. "I guess it's a good thing we came early."

As they pulled into one of the few remaining spots, Mavis' cell phone rang. According to the screen, it was Kim's house phone; maybe her best friend hadn't been able to come after all! She sure wished the girl would have called before now.

"Hello?"

"Ah, Mavis! Hello!" It was Kim's mom. "Sorry to

bug you; I meant to call you earlier. Kim told me you and your friend would be with her and Shawn tonight. I'm hoping that was true."

"We're here right now," Mavis confirmed, relieved. "Kim wouldn't lie to you."

She could hear the woman's sigh of relief. "Good; I can put that out of my mind. Now, you kids have fun, and make sure she gets back here by eleven."

"No problem, even if I have to drag her home myself."

She said goodbye and disconnected the call. Colin waited patiently for her, smiling. She looked at him and rolled her eyes.

"Kim's mom, making sure I'm with her."

Colin laughed. "I see. Ready?"

After her nod, the pair got out of the car. Immediately, oohs and aahs began to flood toward them. She heard several people calling out their names, along with kissing sounds and tons of laughter. Colin looked over at her, and Mavis groaned.

"Let's make it worth their while," he said with a smile.

He put his arm over her shoulders and gave her a peck on the cheek. The strong, beefy smell which was emanating from him quickly reminded her that she had forgotten to put menthol rub in her nose. This whole thing was starting to become a bit exhausting.

Colin held the Sports Burger door open for her, and she smiled a thank you in his direction. "I have to go to the ladies' room," she said. "Will you find Kim and

Shawn? I'll catch up in a minute."

"Sure." Colin waded his way into the crowd of loud teens, while Mavis turned into the restroom area.

The ladies' room was just as packed as the dining area and parking lot. Girls crowded at the mirror and freshened their makeup; others stood in a little group whispering and laughing, while yet another sat with her rear end in one of the sinks, kicking her legs back and forth while she talked to one of her friends. Mavis looked toward the stalls just in time to see a girl come out of the last one with a friend. She shot toward the stall before anyone else could get it.

The room smelled like lightly seasoned roast beef, and Mavis was beginning to get uncomfortable. With shaking hands, she flung the bolt on the stall door, glanced at the toilet, then plopped down. She couldn't get to her menthol rub fast enough. She fumbled around in her purse, nearly dropping it when she pulled it out. The smell of fresh meat was so strong that her shakes were turning into full-blown tremors.

At last, Mavis got the lid off and managed to get a couple smears up her nose. The strong menthol scent soon soaked up the aroma of all the bodies in the room, to her relief. She closed her eyes and inhaled deeply, over and over, until all she could smell was the menthol rub. Now she could join the others.

"There she is!" Kim said as Mavis fought to get to the table. "What took you so long?"

Mavis plopped down in a chair. "The bathroom is a zoo." Turning to Colin, she asked, "Are you ready to order?"

He nodded. "How about you tell me what you want, and I'll go up to the counter. This place is a madhouse."

"Good plan." She went ahead and ordered the Soccer Extravaganza in a super-sized meal, which managed to cause Colin to raise his eyebrows quite a bit. As he got up to head to the counter, Mavis tried to hand him twenty dollars, but he brushed her hand aside and walked away.

She looked at Kim and shrugged. "A true gentleman."

"I guess." Her best friend looked around. "So, according to all of these crazies, there is going to be some kind of fight at Connor Park at eight. Supposed to be between Butch Kennedy and Randy Ochs." She leaned forward conspiratorially. "Should we go?"

Mavis wrinkled her nose. "Uh, no. Who wants to see a couple of Neanderthals beating the crap out of each other in the snow?"

Kim shrugged and sat back. "Just sounded like something to do, is all." She turned to Shawn. "So, are you going up to order, or did you want me to do that for us?"

Shawn seemed to quickly snap out of his daze. "Uh, oh, yeah. What do you want?"

Kim's mouth dropped open. "Same as always, Shawn."

The guy stood up. "Uh, yeah. Sorry."

He left the girls to their own devices. Mavis looked at Kim, a broad smile on her face. "He's not really…

the brightest light bulb in the box, is he?"

Kim gave a long, drawn-out groan. "No, but he sure is a cutie, and he can kiss like a master!"

"Gross!"

Kim began to laugh like a hyena.

Mavis began to notice that people were slowly trickling out of the restaurant. One look out the window told her that cars were lining up to leave the lot. She was relieved; too many people seemed to make her a bit nervous these days.

"So, your mom called my phone just as we got here," Mavis said as Colin approached with a tray of food. He sat down and handed her a super-sized soda.

Kim gave a little sneer. "What did she want?"

"To make sure I was going to be with you." Mavis ripped the end off of her straw wrapper. "So, what did you do that your mother is now requiring a chaperone?"

"Nothing," Kim said, shooting a glance at Colin; he was busy opening his sandwich. "Nothing. Just spent too much time together."

Mavis could immediately tell her friend was lying, but because of Colin's presence, she didn't press the issue. Shawn joined them after a minute, and soon, all four of them were practically stuffing their faces. They really didn't even talk for a full five minutes.

When Mavis was finished, she looked up; all three of her friends were still eating, and they all had lots of food left, as well. They were all looking at her in surprise. She could feel herself blushing.

"That was fast," Colin said with a smile.

Mavis smiled back at him weakly and glanced at Kim. "Um, I was super-hungry, I guess."

Sports Burger was really cleared out by the time they were all finished. The four sat and talked for some time, laughing and telling lame jokes. They also discussed the supposed fight at Connor Park; no one really knew why the two boys were throwing down, but it was an interesting topic of conversation.

At 8:30, Kim suggested they all hop in their respective cars and drive by the park. She was interested in whether anyone was still there if the fight had even taken place at all. In Greenville, those types of confrontations were often planned out but rarely seen through. After a bit of thought and discussion, the group, including Mavis, decided that it really wouldn't hurt to spin through the place and see if they could pick up any extra information.

They left the restaurant in their separate vehicles, heading in the same direction. Unfortunately, they weren't even halfway to their destination when they lost each other in traffic. Mavis expressed to Colin that she wasn't worried; they would hook back up with the other couple when they got to Connor Park.

But, much to her dismay, Connor Park was pretty much deserted by the time she and Colin arrived. It was dark, nearly nine, and no other cars were there at all. Mavis had a funny feeling that Kim had managed to pull a fast one.

"I'd better call her." She fished out her cell and called Kim. The phone rang twice and went to voicemail, so Mavis dialed yet again. The second time, the phone went right to voicemail without ringing at all. She disconnected and looked at Colin.

"I'm going to kill her," she stated flatly. "You know how to get to Zander Point, right?"

Colin nodded and started to leave without further ado. Mavis was steaming; she should have known that Kim would try something like this, even though it was a bit out of character for her. The girl had been a bit different since she started dating Shawn, and Mavis knew that it was nothing more than puppy love and preoccupation, but to sneak around on her like this was just wrong. After all, both Mavis and Kim had given Mrs. Coleman their word.

The pair set out purposefully for Zander Point, radio playing softly in the background as Mavis stewed.

CHAPTER 23

Zander Point managed, pretty successfully, to draw teens and young adults all-year round, as long as the heat in their vehicles worked during the winter. Even as Mavis and Colin approached the peak, they could see four cars, exhausts (and windows) steaming. Mavis strained to make out the vehicles clearly; none of them appeared to be Shawn Maher's rusty heap.

"Look," she said after a minute. "That's Kevin Dorsey's car; pull up to it, will you?"

Colin pulled the sedan in next to a small, newer model red sports car. Mavis jumped out and rapped on the driver's window, which immediately rolled down about six inches. Kevin Dorsey peered at her through the narrow opening, a look of recognition coming over his face.

"Hey, Mavis. What's up?"

Kevin Dorsey was also on the football team, as a backup player. She knew that, since Jeff's death, Shawn and Kevin had sort of clicked a bit. If Shawn and Kim had been there, Kevin would know it.

"Hey, Kevin," she replied, her face serious. "Have Shawn and Kim been up here?"

The boy got a confused look on his face as if he wasn't able to register the question. A few seconds passed, and then his date leaned forward, a girl Mavis recognized from school and knew as Kamryn. She gave a slightly annoyed smile.

"They were here for about twenty minutes, but left pretty fast," she said. "They talked to us for a minute, but she was stressing about someone finding her here, or not finding her here, or something."

"Do you know where they went?"

The girl shrugged and sat back. "They didn't say."

Mavis growled and went back to her car without even so much as a 'thank you.' "They were here, but they left a little while ago. I'm gonna kill her, Colin. She did this on purpose."

He backed out of the parking spot. "Maybe not; maybe it was an accident that we lost them."

"No," Mavis replied with a shake of her head. "Believe me, I know Kim."

They began to head back to the main street. "So, what should we do?"

She thought about it for a minute. "I guess just head back to my house. Sorry about all this."

"No problem."

Mavis reached into her purse and put more menthol rub in her nose; she could smell Colin again, so it was time for a fresh application. Turning up the radio, she pushed Kim and Shawn out of her mind. If Mrs. Coleman asked, she would tell her the truth; it would be Kim's own fault if she got into trouble.

Colin pulled into her driveway. "Thanks for going out with me, and for letting me drive." He started to reach for the key, but Mavis stopped him.

"Thank you for coming with me."

He turned to her, a slightly nervous look on his face. "Well…"

Before she could change her mind, Mavis leaned forward and kissed him, slowly and fully, on the lips. Colin didn't hesitate; he kissed her back, and it was so good that Mavis got light-headed. Without thinking, she wrapped her arms around his neck and started to let herself go. It felt amazing.

Soon, Colin was kissing her cheek, then her ear, then her neck. She buried her own face in his shoulder and let him kiss her, goosebumps breaking out all over her skin. It didn't take long, however, for Mavis to start spinning a bit out of control.

Her mouth began to water first. Next, she began to inhale his scent deeply, not even realizing what she was doing. Mavis was completely unaware of the fact that she was way too close to him, which had rendered her menthol rub pretty much ineffective.

He was a great big steak, a raw T-bone. She inhaled over and over, a bit of drool on her lip. In her mind, she picked up the T-bone, gave it a big whiff, and sank her teeth right into the meatiest part.

"Ow!"

Colin jerked away from her, and his hand shot to his shoulder. Mavis shook her head, trying to clear the fog that had overcome her. Where was she? In her car? Oh, she was with Colin! Had she tried to eat him?

"Wow, Mav," he said with an uncomfortable chuckle. "You really get into it, don't you?"

She ran her hand through her hair and met his eyes. "I'm sorry. I don't know what came over me. I guess I thought I was just… nibbling, or something."

Colin's face relaxed, and he broke into his old, familiar grin. "It's okay."

He started to reach for her again, but this time she dodged him. "Um, I should probably get inside."

He looked hurt for a fraction of a second. "Are you mad or something?"

Mavis smiled, more to comfort him than anything. "No! No, I'm not mad. A little embarrassed, maybe. But not mad. I guess I'm just tired, not to mention mad at Kim. I'm sorry for biting you; I really didn't mean it."

"I understand," Colin replied. "How about a hug?"

Mavis nodded and leaned forward. As he wrapped his arms around her she held her breath; it wouldn't do to get carried away. Obviously, even a fraction of a second was way too dangerous.

They said their goodbyes, and Colin hopped in his truck and left. Mavis hurried into the house and, after locking the doors, changed into an old holey pair of blue jeans and a navy blue t-shirt. She needed to check her traps out back; the moment with Colin in the car had almost sent her spiraling out of control, and her taste for meat was raging overwhelmingly.

There was nothing in her backyard traps, so Mavis ended up eating some liver out of her cooler. The stuff didn't even taste good anymore, and it definitely didn't energize her, like it had in the beginning. The blood managed to appease her craving slightly, which she knew she would have to settle for.

By eleven thirty, Mavis was half-asleep on her bed, a cheesy sitcom playing on her television. When her cell phone rang, it jerked her from her rest, and she sat straight up, wide awake and rigid. A glance at the screen told her it was Kim.

"I'm going to kill you," she said as soon as she answered. "I'm really pissed, Kim. You think you were pissed at me the other day? I'm furious!"

Her friend groaned dramatically into the phone. "I'm sorry, Mav! I knew you wouldn't go for letting us be alone after you had talked to my mom, so…"

Mavis interjected. "So, you lie to me basically, and then sneak off and turn your phone to silent?" Mavis was steaming; she could literally kill her friend right then.

Kim was silent for a second, then replied, "Um… yeah?"

Mavis hung up the phone.

She was changing into pajamas when she heard her parents come into the house, laughing loudly. It sounded to her like either one of them or both of them, were a little drunk, so she turned her television down and locked her bedroom door. She was in no mood to deal with anyone.

When her cell started to ring again, and Mavis saw that it was Kim, she gave the girl a taste of her own medicine and shut off her ringer. She would not be dealing with her parents, and she certainly would not be dealing with the deceptive little Kim. Tomorrow was a new day, and that was when she would pick up and continue with life.

CHAPTER 24

Mavis woke to a light rapping at her bedroom door. Her eyes fluttered open gently, and she listened closely. Soon, the sound came again, but this time her mother's voice quickly followed it.

"Mav? Are you going to sleep all day? Breakfast is ready."

She rubbed her eyes and yawned. "Okay. I'll be out; just give me a few minutes."

"Okay." Jane's footsteps retreated up the hall.

She stared at the ceiling for a bit, then reached for her cell: three missed calls, all from Kim. She wasn't awake enough for it, so she opened her Social Media page and started scrolling, a few seconds before another call from her best friend, and soon-to-be murder victim interrupted her.

"Yes?" She answered the phone with a snappy voice, intending for Kim to know she still wasn't happy with her.

There was a pause. "Hey, Mav. I guess you're still mad, huh?"

Mavis rolled her eyes and sat up in bed, swinging her feet to the floor. "Wouldn't you be? I mean, come on,

Kim. Of all people, I should be the one you'd be honest with, don't you think?"

"Um, yeah."

She just wasn't ready to deal with this. "You know what? I just woke up. I mean, I'm not even out of bed. How about you give me some time to process what a butt you can really be, and I'll call you back."

She hung up on her pal for the second time in less than twelve hours. Mavis had a big, long stretch, then went to lay her phone back on the nightstand. That was when she saw that Colin Handley was calling her. She just couldn't catch a break!

"Hello?"

"Good morning! Are you up and about?" Colin sounded cheerful, but even worse, he sounded wide awake.

She did a mental head slap. "I just now opened my eyes, pretty much."

"Oh!" he paused. "Well, I won't keep you. I just wanted to say that I had a great time last night. I can't wait until we have more time alone... like that. You know?"

"Me too."

"So," he continued. "I'm heading down to the shelter. How's Feisty?"

"He's good, incredible." Oh, she had forgotten to let Feisty out the night before! She hoped he hadn't pooped on the floor; she'd hear about it for a week and be forced to take her back to grandma's house permanently.

"Good. Well, I'll give you a ring later, all right?"

Mavis stifled another yawn. "Sure. Talk to you then."

Once she was finally off the phone, Mavis quickly dressed and brushed her hair. She ignored an extended makeup session and settled on a layer of powder; she needed to tone down her veins a bit. They seemed to be standing out a bit more starkly that morning. The last thing she needed was for her mother to get all riled up over it, especially when Mavis had so much on her mind.

When she was finished, Mavis grabbed her cell and went out to the kitchen. Her father was gone, who knew where, and Jane was at the table reading the paper. The kitchen smelled like bacon and maple syrup.

"Good morning," she greeted as she grabbed a plate from the cupboard and began loading it up.

"Morning," Jane replied. "Hope you slept well."

Mavis plopped down across the table with the food and a glass of milk. "As well as I could; sort of had a frustrating night."

"Hmm," Jane muttered softly. "That's shocking, considering you were thoughtful enough to leave such a precious gift for me to find when I got home."

Mavis stopped chewing and looked up. "Did Feisty poo?"

"Did Feisty poo? That's an understatement."

Mavis glanced out the back door to see the dog prancing around, chasing some unseen thing. "Is it very cold outside?"

Jane shook her head. "No; it's almost forty, which is why he's out there. I'll bring him in shortly. So, things didn't go well with Colin?"

Mavis washed her food down with some milk. "No, Colin was fine. Kim managed to pull a stunt that pissed me off though."

"Mavis!"

She winced. "Sorry, Mom. But she did."

"What did she do?" Jane asked, stepping quickly into gossip mode.

Mavis stabbed at some eggs and ate them. After wiping her mouth, she said, "Well, as you know, Colin and I were going to meet her and Shawn because Mrs. Coleman wants them to ease up on their alone time, right?"

"Right."

Mavis sat back in her chair and crossed her arms over her chest for effect. "Well, it all started off fine. We went and had burgers, then Kim mentioned that these two guys from school were planning to duke it out at Connor Park, and she said she was kind of hip on going."

Jane got a look of amazement on her face. "Boys were going to fight? In the snow in the park? In the dark? And Kim wanted to watch? I swear I don't understand you kids, at all."

"Well," Mavis replied as she grabbed a slice of bacon off her plate, "I didn't want to go. I mean, who wants to watch such stupidity? Anyway, she talked Colin and me into just cruising through Connor to see what we could see, then we were going to do something else. We left in my car, and Kim and Shawn left in his, but when we got to Connor, like fifteen minutes later, there was, like, no one there. No one at all… not even Kim or Shawn."

Jane was hooked. "Where were they?"

Mavis shrugged and chewed her bacon. "Heck, I don't know. I figured they snuck up to Zander Point to sneak some smooches, so Colin and I went up there. They weren't there either, but a classmate and his girlfriend told me they had just left."

"So, what was she doing? Where was she?"

Mavis shrugged again, this time sneering as she recalled trying to call Kim's silenced cell. "I don't know; she ditched me. Basically, she used Colin and me to shut her mom up, then ditched us both."

"No way!"

"Way."

Jane sat back hard, coffee cup in hand. "I can't believe it, Mav. That just doesn't sound like Kim."

"You're telling me?" She drained her milk, then rose to refill her glass. "Anyway, I talked to her after I got home. She called, but I was so mad I ended up hanging up on her. Then when you woke me, I saw I missed three calls from her, but I had shut my phone off like she did to me. She called before I came out for breakfast, though."

Mavis sat back down; Jane was leaning forward eagerly once again. "What did she say? What was her excuse?"

"I wasn't awake enough to talk to her," she replied. "And to be honest, I'm still pissed. I mean, I'm still mad."

Now it was Jane's turn to shrug. "I don't blame you. What the heck is that girl thinking? Do you suppose they're having… sex?"

"Mom!"

"Well!" Jane had a slight smile on her face. She got up and let Feisty in, who ran so fast through the door that when he saw Mavis and tried to stop, he wound up sliding three feet across the tile. The dog jumped up, his front paws on her lap; Mavis gave him a bit of bacon.

"No people food!" Jane exclaimed as she sat down again. "Anyway, don't ever say this to your dad or grandmother, but your father and I were having sex at your age. Why shouldn't Kim? I mean, not that it's right, or I encourage it, but it certainly wouldn't surprise me."

Mavis wanted to choke on her food. "Mother, TMI! That is so gross!"

Jane made a sound like a sexy cat. "It's how you got here."

Her plate was clean, so Mavis put it in the dishwasher. "I'll be right back; I'm going to go call her."

"Tell me what she says," Jane said. "I'm dying to find out."

Mavis went to her room. The first thing she had to do was have some liver. She was feeling drained and tired, and she hadn't felt like that in some time. She locked herself in and ate the last of her stash, then yelled up the hall to Jane that she needed money for the liver for school; Jane acknowledged her.

Now it was time to call Kim. Mavis picked up the phone but hesitated. She wasn't ready to hash it out with her friend, but the issue wasn't going to clear itself up. After a bit, she gave in and called.

Kim picked up on the first ring. "I was hoping you would call soon. I feel bad."

"You should." Mavis wasn't going to pull any punches. "You were mad at me for getting overwhelmed and accidentally blowing you off, then you intentionally do it to me. I'm pissed."

"I know. I'm sorry." Kim sounded sorry, but Mavis wasn't satisfied.

She cleared her throat. "We went to Zander Point, and Kevin Dorsey's girlfriend said you just left; where did you go?"

Kim paused. For a moment, Mavis thought she wasn't going to answer, but finally, she did. "To Shawn's."

Mavis was confused. "Shawn's?"

"Yeah," Kim replied. "His, uh, parents weren't home. So…"

"Are you two having sex, Kim?" Mavis just laid the question on the line; she was sick of going around and around the mulberry bush with her friend.

Kim didn't answer.

"Kim, I asked you if you and Shawn are doing the deed! Are you?" Now Mavis sounded mad, and she knew it.

When the girl answered, her voice was so low Mavis barely could hear her. "Sort of."

"Sort of?" Mavis was shocked beyond belief. Not that her friend was having sex, but that the girl hadn't told her. "There is no sort of! Either you are, or you aren't!"

"Okay, okay!" Kim exclaimed. "Yes, we are!"

Mavis flopped back on her bed as the breath left her body. What the heck was going on? Mavis could think of one thing to say.

"I hope you are using protection. I have to go."

She hung up the phone again. Mavis felt tears stinging her eyes; life was passing too fast, and she felt like she couldn't keep up. So much had changed since junior year started that Mavis' head was spinning. What would she tell her mom when she asked for an update? She couldn't really lie to her about something like that; Jane would see right through her! If she told the truth, Mrs. Coleman would know before Mavis was even done relaying the information.

Mavis felt sick. She thought she might puke for a moment, but the feeling passed. The truth was, Kim was a big girl, and her own person; she would do as she pleased. If Mavis really loved her and were a true friend, she would stick by her side no matter what.

Mavis redialed the number.

"Hey, I'm okay. I forgive you for ditching me."

CHAPTER 25

There was one full week left before the big Winter Formal, and the excitement of the upcoming dance was tangible in the hallways of Westside High School.

For Mavis, the week proved to be packed full of things to do. First, her dress was delivered that Monday. After school, Mavis had dropped Kim off at home, but as soon as she got home and her mother handed her the package, she called her best friend, who already had gotten hers. They planned to get together after Mavis ate something and took Feisty for a walk; that way, they could try on the dresses and discuss their shoes and accessories. Mavis was a step ahead of Kim, however. She had the shawl she planned to wear to cover her shoulders, but she also had her shoes and a clutch purse chosen.

Jane had frozen pizza cooking; while it finished baking, Mavis took Feisty out and walked him around the block a couple of times, making sure to pick up his poo, since he did his business in front of crabby old Mrs. Channing around the block. When she got home, the pizza was ready, and Mavis was more than ready to stuff her face. By five she had her things in the car and was ready to leave for Kim's house; Mavis planned to have supper there, as well.

Twenty minutes later, she was sitting comfortably on Kim's bedroom floor, waiting for Mrs. Coleman to yell down the hall and announce supper. The pizza she had eaten was long forgotten already. Mavis was actually very excited to get to eat someone else's cooking for once, not that she would have ever told her mother that.

Thankfully, dinner was served before the girls even tried on their dresses. An eager Mavis found herself highly disappointed, but she didn't let on. Supper at Kim's ended up being Mrs. Coleman's homemade version of ground beef helper. While it didn't taste bad, it did nothing for Mavis' blood or raw meat cravings, and even though her stomach was packed full by the time the meal was over, the desire for satisfaction was nagging at both her belly and her brain.

With the meal finished, the girls headed back to try on their dresses. Mavis ended up changing into hers in the bathroom, telling Kim she had to pee anyway, so she would just change in there. But the truth was that she was intent on hiding her veins and gray spots, and putting the dress on in the bathroom was the one safe way to do that.

While she changed, she thought about Kim not telling her about crossing the line with Shawn. She hadn't brought it up since she had arrived, but she certainly intended to before she left. As she pondered what method she would use to broach the subject, something occurred to her that she hadn't considered before.

Kim had, for the first time in their nearly life-long relationship, kept some pretty significant information from her: she was having sex. Mavis was hurt that Kim hadn't talked to her about it, but deep inside she understood why. It hurt her feelings that Kim felt uncomfortable talking to her, no matter how the girl was afraid she would react, and that was something Mavis didn't get.

But then, as she sat on the closed lid of the toilet putting her strappy heels on, something came to Mavis, and it hit her pretty hard indeed. Hadn't she, herself, been keeping some pretty heavy stuff from her best friend as well? Hadn't Mavis been keeping secrets? Yes! She had in no way told her friend about her urges or rapidly growing taste for… meat. She hadn't confided in her best friend about Jeff, or about the traps, or the liver, or anything. She wasn't about to.

Deep inside, Mavis knew that there was no way Kim would understand… murder. A murder was exactly what Mavis had committed. Jeff Deason, the first boy she had ever had feelings of any kind for in her life.

No, Kim would never understand; it was best that Mavis not tell her.

But that didn't mean she couldn't be more understanding toward her friend because of it, and she intended to. Because of her own secrets, Mavis should perfectly understand why Kim would be apprehensive about telling her about having sex. Her best friend more than likely had been worried that Mavis would be disappointed, and she had been.

But she also knew that Kim would be disappointed if she found out that Mavis liked to snack on everyday people, for sure.

She left the bathroom, adjusting to the black heels she had chosen to wear with the dress. To Mavis' relief, neither Kenny, Kim's brother, nor her friend's parents, were in sight, so they didn't get a load of her wobbling up the hall. Considering that she was afraid of falling on her face, their absence was a load off.

"Well," Mavis exclaimed as she walked into Kim's room, "what do you think?"

Kim was struggling to zip her zipper, which was on the side of the dress. She looked up, and a smile came over her face. "Perfect! Now come help me get this stupid zipper, will you?"

Mavis wobbled over to her friend, and in a few seconds, she had the zipper up. The girls stood side by side, looking in the massive mirror that entirely made up one of Kim's sliding closet doors. They observed themselves in silence, smiles on their faces.

After a moment, Mavis said, "I love it."

"Me too," Kim mumbled. "Why are you wearing that shawl? You did that at homecoming, too. What's the deal?"

Mavis shrugged and turned away from the mirror, plopping down on Kim's bed to remove her shoes. "Well, my skin has gotten so pale from the anemia that you can see my veins. So, I guess I just want to camouflage as much as possible, you know?"

"Oh, I get it," her friend replied as she kicked her own black pumps off. "I guess I didn't know what was happening. You pull it off really well, Mav."

Mavis gave a sarcastic chuckle. "Thanks, but it wears on the self-esteem if you know what I mean."

With her shoes off, Kim sat down in her desk chair and studied Mavis for a moment. "Mav, I'm sorry I didn't tell you about Shawn and me. I guess I knew how you'd respond, so I procrastinated. It wasn't that I didn't trust you at all."

Mavis looked at Kim and smiled. "Well, you didn't trust me. So, I was disappointed, but I was more upset that you ditched me, and that made my reaction worse." She continued to study her friend, who obviously felt bad. "I forgive you, so now we can drop it. But…"

"But what?" Kim pressed.

Mavis sighed. "I think you should talk to your mom. I mean, are you using birth control? Are you guys responsible? I mean, I like Shawn, I really do, but we both know he's not that bright. You have to take responsibility for yourself and your health."

"Oh! I can't tell my mom!" Kim looked stricken at the suggestion.

Mavis didn't really push, she just encouraged. "Kim, you have to. She might freak at first, but in the end, she's going to be thankful that you trusted her enough to go to her and be honest. If you don't, and she finds out some other way, it's going to break her heart."

Kim was starting to get tears in her eyes.

"Look," Mavis continued. "I promise, I won't

interfere; you don't have to worry about that. But please just think about it; if and when you decide to do it, I'll be with you, if you want. That way you don't have to face it alone."

Kim nodded slightly and brushed at a falling tear. "I'll think about it; I promise."

Mavis headed back for the bathroom and changed back into her street clothes, then took the dress back into Kim's room and gently put it, along with her shawl and tights, back into the box. She hung out a bit longer, talking about other things so Kim wouldn't be stressed when she left. They discussed midterms, and what kind of grades they thought they were going to pull on them. Kim had major anxiety about Calculus, but otherwise, she seemed confident. Mavis wasn't worried about any of her tests, but she pretended to be concerned about social studies for her best friend's sake. She didn't want Kim to feel alone when it came to her concern for the midterm results.

By 8:30, Mavis was on her way home. She pulled into the driveway to see Jane standing in the front yard wearing footie pajamas with boots over them and a winter coat. She had Feisty on a leash and was begging him to pee.

"How did it fit?" she asked as soon as Mavis was out of the car. "Does it look amazing?"

"Yes! I love it! Thanks, Mom." She crossed the yard through the snow, arms laden with the box, her purse, and her heels. Mavis planted a kiss on her mother's cheek. "If you take this stuff, I'll finish up with Feisty."

"I've got it," Jane replied. "Don't go to bed though; we'll gab awhile."

Mavis agreed, and she went inside to put her things away and get changed into something more comfortable. She didn't have any homework to focus on since it was nearing the very end of the semester, so she was eager to spend a bit of time with her mom. Since she had gotten older, they had become pretty good friends.

They sat at the table with hot cocoa in their cups, talking about the upcoming dance with Feisty sleeping on his dog bed in the corner. After many jokes and laughter, Mavis began to get a bit somber. It seemed she couldn't stop worrying about Kim, and she made a decision to talk to her mother about it. She was a bit worried Jane would call Mrs. Coleman, so she also chose to tell her that Kim was going to do it herself the following day. Mavis just wanted to know how her mother would react because it would be a good indicator of what Kim should expect from her own mom.

"Mavis, what's on your mind?" Jane picked up on her change of mood almost immediately.

Mavis shrugged and stroked the lip of her cocoa cup with her thumb. "Well, it's Kim… sort of."

Jane didn't respond; true to form, once she knew Mavis had a serious issue, she waited patiently. It was one of her mother's qualities that she admired the most. When she had children someday, Mavis hoped she was as open and eager to listen as Jane always was.

"Um, we kind of had a falling out last weekend over her ditching me," Mavis began.

Jane sipped her cocoa. "I knew that. Are you two still on the outs?"

Mavis shook her head. "No, we cleared it up; I forgave her and all. But that's not the issue."

She paused so she could think through her wording, but Jane was on top of things already.

"So, she's having sex," Jane said suddenly as if it were common knowledge. "I take it you've encouraged her to go to her mother?"

Mavis stared, open-mouthed, at her mom. "How did you know?"

With a shrug, Jane replied, "I was your age once like I said before. Your dad and I…"

Mavis held up her hand to stop her mother. "I know, I know. Yes, I told her she has to talk to her mom. I also agreed to be with her; she is supposed to think about it. You're not going to call Mrs. Coleman, are you?"

Jane shook her head. "Of course not, but I certainly hope she does it. It would hurt her mom terribly to find out on her own, or to find out because Kim wound up… pregnant."

"Right."

Her mother studied her. "So, why is it bothering you?"

"I'm not sure," Mavis replied thoughtfully. "I just want her to do the right thing, for herself."

"Me too."

They talked a bit longer, then around midnight, they turned in. Mavis wasn't worried about being tired at school the following day. She knew that classes were going to be very laid back that week.

After snacking on a piece of liver, Mavis snuggled down for the night.

CHAPTER 26

Mavis found herself in a spectacular mood as soon as she opened her eyes on Tuesday morning.

She hummed while she dressed and did her makeup, and she chattered all through breakfast. Any break from school, whether it be winter or summer break, always managed to give Mavis' heart wings, and this year was no exception. Just four more days until both the dance and winter break. The dawn of the new day and the nearness of freedom had her dancing on air.

She ate so much for breakfast and chowed down on enough liver in her room that she blew off checking her traps that morning. With all the stuff going on with Kim, Mavis felt that it was better for her to put her friend first. She showed up at Kim's door; she didn't want the girl to take off walking for school, but she wanted to surprise her, so being early was imperative.

"What are you doing here?" The look on Kim's face consisted of both surprise and confusion.

Mavis innocently shrugged. "I don't have any extra stuff to do, what with the holiday vacation being so close. Besides, I miss riding to school with my favorite sidekick."

The girls climbed into the car and took off. About a block up the road, Kim turned down the radio as if she wanted to talk, but initially, she said nothing. Mavis waited as long as she could without dying of curiosity before she spoke up herself.

"What's going on?"

Kim sighed. "I thought I should tell you: I told my mother this morning."

Mavis nearly sent them flying through the windshield, she hit the brakes so hard. A car behind her began to honk angrily, so she pulled over to the curb. Her heart was pounding at Kim's revelation.

After putting the car in park, she asked gently, "What did she say?"

Kim smiled. "Nothing. Believe it or not, she wasn't mad or freaked out at all. She said not to talk to dad about it, but she is making a doctor appointment for me today, so we can discuss birth control and all that."

Mavis couldn't contain her pleasure. "Oh, Kim! I'm so relieved." Undoing her seat belt, she leaned over and gave her friend a long, suffocating hug. "I knew it would be okay; I knew it!"

"Yeah, and she was happy I was honest." Kim chuckled. "She said she already knew, and she was worried sick, but me coming to her made it better. Now we can deal with things in a mature, responsible manner, she said."

Mavis sat back, a cheesy smile glued to her face. "She's right, Kim."

The girl looked at her. "I know. Thanks, Mav. I'm

so sorry."

Mavis held up her hand. "Don't. It's over."

She pulled away once again, and Kim turned the radio up. All the way to school, the girls sang along with the song that was playing, a poppy number seasoned with a bit of rap. Even though Mavis' taste was leaning drastically toward heavy metal, she thought that Kim deserved to hear what she wanted, so she let it fly.

It was amazing how much stress was relieved for them both, and it showed.

∞

"Mavis, I really want you to go out with me on Friday night."

Colin and Mavis were in Calculus, which Mr. Jacobi had graciously turned into an open hour. Kids were milling around, playing cards, or scrolling through their phones. Colin was sitting at the desk in front of Mavis', turned around so they could talk.

"I don't know, Colin," she replied.

He gave her a grumbling sound. "Listen, Mav, we're going to the dance together. It will be fine! We can catch a movie, then do whatever you want. Come on, give me a break here!"

Mavis thought about it. For the last few days, Mavis' urges for blood and raw meat had seemed to be under control; maybe things were easing up for her. Not to mention the fact that he was right: they didn't go out ever. What would a movie hurt?

"Fine," she said at last, with a smile. "A movie sounds good anyway."

Colin pumped his fist in the air. "Yes!" he exclaimed. "What do you want to see?"

"Surprise me."

The bell rang loudly, interrupting Colin's seeming ecstasy. When they left class, he walked her to Kim's locker, where her best friend was waiting for her. Colin felt the need to fill Kim in as soon as they saw her.

"Mavis agreed to go out with me Friday night!" he said.

Kim raised her eyebrow at her friend. "Really? It's about time; after all, you two are going to the ball together. I don't know what took you so long."

Mavis shrugged, a smile on her face. "Things, I guess... just things."

Colin kissed her on the cheek. "We'd better get to class or all three of us will be heading to the office for passes. See you later, Mav."

"Later," she replied with a smile.

She and Kim started off down the hall. "I have to say, I'm glad you are going. It's about time you started to move on from Jeff."

Typically, Mavis didn't have time for statements like that, even from her own mother. No one knew the real story behind Jeff's dying, and she didn't feel like they should be making assumptions. But what else were they supposed to do? Besides, today she didn't feel any kind of animosity, and the fact that she had been the one to kill Jeff seemed like some kind of bad dream for the first time since it had happened.

She dropped Kim at her French class, then headed

for German. She knew they were going to be playing 'German Hangman' all period, and she was almost eager to participate in the game. Mavis loved how laid back the entire week was going to be.

∞

After school, while they were getting in the car, Kim told Mavis that her mother had texted her.

"I have an appointment at Dr. Meadows at four," Kim revealed. "I have to get right home and get a quick shower."

So, the girls didn't dawdle. Mavis got her to her house, then steered the car toward her own home. When she got there, her mother's car was warming up in the driveway, and she found Jane inside putting on her coat.

"What's up, lady?" she asked as she removed her own jacket.

Jane groaned. "I have to fill in at the food bank for Helen Mead. There are pizza rolls in the freezer, and Feisty needs to be walked. I just got the call, or I would have taken care of him myself." Jane grabbed her purse off the entryway table. "I'll be home by six, so supper will be late."

"Do you want me to get it started?" Mavis asked.

Jane thought for a moment. "We're just having burgers and fries, so it can wait. But you can certainly help me when I do cook." She kissed her daughter on the cheek and opened the door to leave. "See you soon."

"I have a date on Friday with Colin," Mavis

suddenly gushed.

Jane froze in the doorway and turned around. "Now, why did you have to bring that up now? Mavis, it's going to drive me crazy until I get home. Thanks!"

Mavis laughed as her mother rushed out. After Jane was gone, Mavis quickly changed into a sweatsuit, then put some pizza rolls into the oven. Instead of walking Feisty, Mavis took him out back with her and tossed his ball around until he did his business. At one point she thought about checking her traps and even started for the thicket, but as she neared it, Mavis realized that she wasn't really craving any bloody food. She decided to check it later if the need arose.

Maybe she was getting better after all.

CHAPTER 27

The rest of the last week before winter break went extremely smoothly for Mavis and the rest of the student body. They wasted their class time playing games and talking, with each and every teacher's participation and approval. The freedom had everyone feeling like they were on top of the world.

Before she knew it, Friday had arrived. Mavis had pondered her pending date with Colin countless times over the last several days, waiting for a feeling of fear or dread to come, but none ever did. When coupled with the fact that regular food, a random trap surprise, and raw liver seemed to be keeping her violent cravings away, Mavis was nearly convinced that things were looking up for her health-wise. She attributed her lack of date-night nerves to that specifically.

During both Calculus and German Colin hovered over her, excitedly talking about the movie he had picked, which was some popular new comedy. His excitement was contagious, and the more he discussed the evening, the more psyched up Mavis got. She even found herself considering her clothing for the date, mentally changing her mind a thousand times.

As for Kim, she had her appointment at the doctor on Tuesday afternoon and wound up getting a birth control implant. Now she was able to be alone with Shawn all she wanted without giving Mrs. Coleman ulcers or a heart attack. Things seemed to be lightening up all around.

∞

After school, Kim chose to ride home with Shawn, so Colin, who had to attend a short training session at the humane shelter, walked Mavis to her car.

"So, I'll pick you up at seven," he told her as she buckled in. "The movie starts at 7:40, so we'll have time to get food and find good seats. Sound good?"

"Perfect," she replied.

He bent over and kissed her, then closed her car door securely. During the drive home, it occurred to Mavis that the menthol rub had been working quite well. She hadn't been distracted by Colin smelling like raw beef in more than a week, and it made her feel more secure than ever about their date.

She went home and walked Feisty, then hung out in the kitchen with her mother and stuffed her face with a warmed-up hamburger on a pretzel bun and some French fries. They talked about what she was going to wear on her date, the movie they would be seeing, and what she would be doing for supper. Mavis reassured Jane that they would grab a bite after the movie, so she had nothing to worry about.

She also told her mom that she felt better than ever and that she thought her anemia was improving. Jane was glad to hear it, and her mood even seemed lighter after she heard, if that was at all possible. While they talked, large snowflakes began to fall to the ground, and they also talked about the fact that they were supposed to get several inches. Mavis reassured her mother that they would be taking Colin's truck to the movie, which also made her mother very happy.

At five, Mavis jumped in the shower and took her time scrubbing up. She enjoyed the hot water immensely and was in no rush to get out. So, she spoiled herself by dawdling, washing her hair and soaping up two full times.

For her date, she decided to veer off the beaten path. Instead of all black, she opted to wear blue jeans and a sweater. Colin would be pleased to see her in something with a little bit of color.

Mavis had been doing a lot of thinking about Kim and the sex thing. She had been doing so much thinking about it that she found herself considering her own sex life or lack thereof. She decided that, if Colin was game, tonight would be the night they would talk about it.

She wanted to go to go all the way with Colin Handley, and if all went well, she would ask her mom for a birth control implant.

By the time she had herself together, it was nearly six thirty. Mavis sat at the kitchen table talking to her parents while they ate, and before she knew it, the doorbell was ringing. She went to answer it, with both Todd and Jane on her heels. It was time for Colin to meet her mom and dad, obviously.

"Hey, Colin!" Mavis stood back and let him in. "This is my mom Jane, and my dad Todd."

Todd reached out and shook Colin's hand, and Jane asked, "What are you two seeing?"

Colin shrugged. "A movie called *Bird Feathers* with that comedian Blastin' Bob in it. It's supposed to be funny."

"Sounds good," Todd said. "Well, hopefully, we get some time to talk and get to know each other better; you two have fun."

Before Mavis knew it, they were off to the movie. They sat holding hands in the truck all the way there. When they got to the theater, they managed to load up on food, and they even found great seats in the packed room.

Mavis knew it was going to be a great night.

The movie was hilarious. Mavis laughed so hard she nearly spit food out of her mouth on more than one occasion. Colin thought she was the cutest thing he had ever seen.

When they finally left the theater, the snow had really built up, and the temperature had dropped. Colin started the truck and let it warm up while they sat. Initially, there was an expectant silence, like they were both trying to figure out what to do next.

At last, Colin made a suggestion. "So, where do you want to eat?"

Mavis gave him a sly smile. "Um, I thought we should go to a drive-thru, and then find some place to be alone…"

Colin smiled back. "Are you saying what I think you're saying? Because if you are, my parents just happen to be in Cincinnati for the weekend."

"Really?" Mavis asked, her eyes lighting up. "Do you have any... anything?"

His smile grew. "Yeah, embarrassingly enough, I do."

"Sports Burger and go?"

Colin didn't even answer; he put the truck into gear and took off.

They stopped at Sports Burger, then made their way to Colin's house. It turned out to be a very nice place, clean and stylish, with very new-looking furniture. Colin put a video in, and the two ate and watched television.

That's when the kissing began.

At first, everything was fine. Their kisses were timid for a bit, but it didn't take long for both of the teens to begin getting worked up. Soon, they were all over each other, their hands roaming and their breathing elevating to outright panting.

Suddenly, Mavis could smell beef.

It all happened very quickly. One minute, the two of them were making out, with Colin's hand up her shirt and her own groping his 'unmentionables.' She was so excited she could barely stand it, and the smell of him had her literally beside herself with excitement.

Then, she came to.

When the fog cleared, Mavis was sitting cross-legged on the living room floor. She was covered in blood, and Colin was lying lifeless on the floor in front of her. He was literally ripped open at the stomach, and Mavis had some of his rib bones clean of flesh. She was smacking her lips sickly as the reality of the situation came to her.

Gosh darn it, she had done it again. She had eaten another boyfriend, much to her dismay. There would be no Winter Formal for Mavis and Colin that year.

Mavis waited until her head was clear. Distraught, she took a towel from the kitchen, dampened it, and wiped her face clean. Next, while averting her eyes from Colin's bloody corpse, she wiped down all she could remember touching. She then tossed the towel to the floor, wrapped her trench coat tightly around her, and left through the back door, careful not to leave any prints.

She walked the eight blocks to her house in a state of confusion and grief. Yep, she had done it again, but wow had it been delicious. Once again, she felt bad that someone had died, not that she had been the one to do it.

The house was dark when she arrived. Quietly, she let herself in, then went right to her room. She stripped off her clothes and put them in the bag lining her wastepaper basket. Tying it off, she put it behind her bedroom door to take out the following day.

She would shower quietly; it wouldn't do to wake her parents.

Mavis felt like a million bucks, energized and clear-headed. She lay in bed and reflected on the flavor of Colin; it had been wonderful. She knew there would be police and interviews, but not until Sunday night at the earliest.

After a while, she fell into a deep sleep, and she had no dreams.

R.W.K. Clark

CHAPTER 28

Even though Colin wouldn't be discovered until Sunday night, Mavis' award-winning acting began on Saturday night, when Colin 'didn't show' to pick her up for the ball.

She went through the motions of getting dressed up and made up, feigning excitement for a night she knew would never happen. Mavis even went through the pain of talking to Kim on speakerphone while they both got ready. All of the pretenses were exhausting, but it was only the beginning.

At seven, she began to pace, her parents exchanging glances. By 7:30 Mavis was dialing Colin's phone over and over. Around 8:15 she was calling him every name in the book, crying hysterically, and changing out of her clothes. She even laid it on thick when Kim called to find out why she was late for the ball.

Once again, Jane loaded her daughter up on sedatives and put her to bed, but not before taking Mavis' phone and calling Colin over and over like a crazy person. Jane was pissed that this was happening to her daughter for the second time in a year, and Colin seemed like such a nice boy. She swore she would wring his neck the next time she saw him.

By Sunday afternoon, Colin had been found. His parents returned home earlier than expected, and there he was, dead and mutilated on the living room floor. When Mavis heard, she flew into hysterics. Even though she knew what happened, getting the news set it in stone, just like last time.

But now she didn't feel as much grief. As a matter of fact, she didn't have any guilt at all. He had been so good that she thought more about his taste than she did about the fact that she had killed and eaten him. The act seemed both reasonable and normal; she simply had to keep up the appearance of being heartbroken if she didn't want to go to prison.

Police interviews followed, but there was no suspicion in regard to Mavis. Greenville police were beginning to think that Mavis had a jealous stalker and that anyone who tried to date her was going to pay the price. It was a new direction for their investigation, and one they intended to follow.

As far as her second victim, Colin Handley? He had been very cute, and pretty fun. But most of all, he had tasted ten times better than she remembered Jeff Deason tasting.

∞

School classes reconvened on January fourth. There was a memorial held for Colin of course, which Mavis cried hysterically through. While she cried, though, she thought about how she would keep herself from doing it yet again. She had some pretty darn good ideas.

It didn't take long for things to pretty much get back to normal. Soon, they were attending classes as usual, and after another month, the death of Colin Handley became a fading topic. Life went on for everyone.

But Mavis was anything but normal. As a matter of fact, she made a firm decision that she wouldn't deprive herself of that yummy meat anymore.

Mavis could hardly wait.

ENTREATY

This book was made possible by reviews from readers like you. Reviews fuel my creativity. If you enjoyed this novel, I implore you to please write a review and share your experience on the retailer's website. The livelihood for authors is entirely dependent on reviews, and I must say, it is the largest obstacle as a struggling author that I have encountered. Please tell a friend, tell a loved one about this read. With your help, I will be one step closer to overcoming this obstacle. In return, I thank you from the bottom of my heart, and sincerely appreciate your time and effort.

Humbled, with gratitude,

R.W.K. Clark

ABOUT THE AUTHOR

I am a father of two beautiful children, Jon and Kim. They are my motivating forces; they are the lighthouse in this vast ocean. In my life, they are the air that I breathe; they are the oasis in this desert of uncertainty. They are my greatest joy in life and my number one priority. I have a long list of hobbies, and I attribute that to my lust for life! I like to surround myself with positive people, who share the same interests. Family values, the arts, outdoors, nature, and travel are tops on my list. I embrace attending cultural and artistic events because I believe dramatic self-expression is the window to the soul. I wear my heart on my sleeve, and I still believe in chivalry, and I always treat people the way I want to be treated.

www.rwkclark.com

www.ingramcontent.com/pod-product-compliance
Lightning Source LLC
Chambersburg PA
CBHW030303200626
46816CB00002BA/737